NECK PAIN

Short Stories by
Matt Gibson

For Poppop.

Contents

Pump it up, Red.

—SLICE

The Plan

It was around seven o'clock, the daylight fading.

Paul was driving how he liked to live, making a game of it.

The freeway was a puzzle.

"What's the move here?" asked Dennis.

Paul grabbed his iPhone, scrolling through his music. "What do you wanna hear?"

"The plan."

Paul ignored him and played *You Don't Need to Laugh* by Frankie Miller.

"We'll get there, we'll park the car—"

"Need more beers," said Paul.

"Okay, so, liquor store. Then we go there."

"That's where we're at, yea."

"Can you stop?"

"That's all we need to think about, Dennis."

"Who's gunna be there? Katie and her crowd going?"

Paul turned Frankie up. "What kind of psychotic fuck can stay in one lane for forty-five minutes? Find the gaps, people. Do some weaving."

Dennis dialed down the music. "You think this is gunna be a backyard thing, or inside?"

"Can you just fucking *be* for a moment?"

"Okay, Confucius."

Paul swigged his beer, then shut Frankie off. "You're like someone in their forties. You really are, you know that? Everything has to be all laid out for you so you can avoid any sort of fucking surprise. God forbid we walk into something not knowing what's gunna happen. Would that kill you? Would it hurt so much to just let things come to you instead of knowing a list of every person that's attending and whether we're gunna be inside or outside and what calculated-yet-somehow-still-awkward shit you're gunna say to Katie when we walk in?"

"Are you done?"

"No, because I don't think you understand. Having everything all plotted out is basically the same thing as being old. Knowing what's coming at you, having a fucking routine all the time, it's not fun. Do you get that?"

Dennis took a moment to respond. "Yea."

"This shit happens slowly. It creeps in. First you get some kind of bullshit job, the first couple months are fine, but then your days start to look familiar. And then you get used to that. And then suddenly you *are* the routine. You start to believe that shit's good for you."

"You know how I am," said Dennis.

"I know, but I wish that sometimes you'd just let it fly."

Dennis sipped his beer. "Sorry."

"Trust me, you'll be one of these fucks soon enough. You'll be in a suit on this exact highway, spending two hours a day in the same lane, staring at the same bumper, thinking about how Paul made so much sense on that one night back in your twenties and how that shit you said to Katie *was* awkward."

Dennis laughed, then laughed harder.

"How easy is that to imagine?" asked Paul.

"Too easy," said Dennis.

"No need to plan that one out. It's set in stone." Paul turned Frankie back on, this time louder. "This the exit?"

Dennis nodded.

"You'll be a corporate tycoon," said Paul, quickly changing lanes.

"Hopefully," said Dennis. The beam of a headlight lit up his face.

"And I'll be—"

El Quetzal

"Is it okay for you if I buy some cocaína?" He did a snorting motion to clarify.

"Of course," I answered.

This—how quickly I was willing to hop on board with this, and almost anything—is a real wild card for most people. They love it or they hate it. The ones who hate it are most people, the majority. They wouldn't be in this situation in the first place.

It was a Tuesday night around 6:00 p.m., and Hector, the new security guard at our office, had invited me to hang out in spectacular fashion. "I need to be up here tonight," he'd said, gesturing upward. "Do you want to join me...*en el cielo?*"

Upon Googling *cielo* and finding out it meant *sky,* I recommended that we get things started immediately. Hector had a bit of prophet about him. What awaited us in the sky? The inquiry had a deeply existential ring to it. This could very well concern the underlying fabric of reality. I also knew, of course, that *the sky* could have just been code for getting high. But that's secondary. The question is always more important than the answer. Always. It's the wondering that makes up a good human life. And Hector had me wondering. Whether his question was philosophical or pharmaceutical in nature, I was in.

Our celestial quest started in a small shed in Hector's backyard. It was a man cave of sorts, but also a workstation—a sawdust-covered love seat, a mini-fridge, a woodworking bench littered with roach clips. The stereo played Hispanic rap, a few screws and bottle caps rattling on top of it.

"It is my uncle house," said Hector. "He always wants to go to the beach. If he comes here to the shed, my uncle, he will ask us if we go to the beach. But here is what we do to him. We will tell him this is break. We are working, and this is our break, only. We will go back to work."

"It'll be dark soon though," I said. "Why does he want to go to the beach?"

"I don't know. He loves the beach. I also. I love it. But my uncle, he does not drink."

I laughed. I couldn't understand if Hector didn't want to go to the beach because it was nighttime or because going with a sober person was unthinkable. "Why doesn't he drink?"

"I don't know." Hector shook his head with utter disappointment. "Qué lástima," he whispered. *What a shame.* He spent about thirty seconds ruminating. I think he was imagining what life would be like entirely sober, and that very terrifying thought made him chase its opposite.

"Is it okay for you if I buy some cocaína?" asked Hector. He did a snorting motion to clarify.

"Of course," I answered.

Hector plopped down on the love seat and started texting his cocaine dealer.

"We call that *getting a close look at the table*," I said.

"What table? This?" asked Hector, touching the slanted workbench. His English was about three-quarters fluent, so there was still a wonderful gap in communication, especially when it came to specific phrases or metaphors or any kind of jargon.

"No, no. La cocaína," I said. "When you do the cocaine, me and my friends, we like to say that *you are getting a close look at the table*." I bent over the table and stared at it, then snorted an invisible line.

A sly grin came to Hector's face as he figured out what I meant. "I like the tables."

Someone knocked on the door.

"¿Qué pasa?" asked Hector. *What's up?*

"¿Quieres ir a la playa?" asked Hector's uncle. *Do you want to go to the beach?*

"No," said Hector. "We are doing a look at the table."

We were speeding down Avalon.

"The police, they never catch me," said Hector. "I am watching." His eyes darted to every mirror. I admired his optimism, but we were red-eyed, ten beers deep, and doing eighty-five in a forty. If we were going to avoid the law, it would be luck that saved us.

"We need some more beers," I said. "And food. We should eat something."

Hector nodded, then fetched a gun from the back pocket of the passenger seat.

"You keep that in here all the time?"

"Yes, I must. You do not know when."

"When what?"

"When they come," he said. "Those motherfuckers."

"Where'd you get that?" I asked.

"A place. A real place," he said, slipping the gun back into the seat. "It has the papers. For my gun, I have the good papers. But for me? I don't have the papers."

We broke into laughter as Hector entered a parking lot with a convenience store and a hole-in-the-wall restaurant. "You buy beers," he said. "I buy pupusas."

I got back into the car with thirty beers and started drinking one while Hector was inside the restaurant. In surveying the area, I could tell this was a good, sketchy parking lot. People sat in their cars waiting, drinking, incessantly checking their phones. *Drugs are here*, that's what I remember thinking when a car pulled up beside me and a man hopped out. He popped his trunk, filled with cooking supplies and beverages. When Hector seamlessly exited the restaurant and started helping the guy carry stuff inside, I joined them. This is a major theme among my Hispanic friends—they help each other carry stuff. At its core, it's kindness. A lot of Americans, myself included, too often default to verbal kindness when the most concise and generous thing you can do is get off your ass and move some shit. Giving a friend a Hallmark card is nice. Helping him move his pool table is saintly.

After a few minutes we'd lugged all the tortillas and vegetable oil and sodas into the small lobby area of the restaurant. It wasn't until the work was done, when the man was shutting his trunk, that Hector even introduced me.

"This is my friend," said Hector. "He has the restaurant."

"Nice to meet you," I said.

The man nodded, smiled, and pointed to a bumper sticker on the back of his car. It was a bird of some kind. A parrot, maybe. "You know this?" he asked, gesturing to an identical one on Hector's car.

"No. What is it?"

"El quetzal," he said.

"That's the type of bird? El quetzal?"

He nodded. "It means Guatemala."

"Best country," added Hector as the two of them entered the restaurant. I followed them, but when I got inside the lobby area they were nowhere to be found. Out of the corner of my eye, I thought I saw them disappear into a doorway, but I couldn't be sure. I approached, peering in. It was the kitchen. A Guatemalan chef just on the verge of midget status was turning over a couple pupusas on the stove. He calmly set down his spatula and walked my way, passing me on his way to the exit. He lit a cigarette, holding the door open for me as if he already knew I'd be leaving: "You are not here."

"What?" I asked.

"This is not you," he said.

I pointed to all the shit we'd carried in, trying to insinuate that I had a friend here, but it was no use. The beautiful language barrier, mother to a billion uncertainties. Words were no good here.

15

"Lost," he said.

I was on my fourth beer when Hector got back into the car.

"Where'd you go?" I asked.

"I order pupusas. And my friend who is in the restaurant, he sells the tables." He reached into his pocket and pulled out a baggie of cocaine.

"Makes sense," I said. I told you it was a good parking lot.

"And he had some extra stuff for us," added Hector, rummaging through his pockets. He grew increasingly more frantic as he searched. Out came his phone, his wallet, a knife, a second smaller knife, a screwdriver, and a bag of weed. Turning his pockets inside out, he realized he'd dropped it, whatever it was.

"What did you lose?"

"Qué lástima," he whispered.

"What was it?"

"Metanfetamina."

"Where do you think you dropped it?"

He pointed back inside the restaurant.

"I'll find it," I volunteered casually. Hector was taken aback when I stepped out of the car. I could have said more to explain myself, to clarify why I wanted to take the risk, but the language barrier probably would have thrown a wrench in my attempt to tell him that hunting for a bag of meth in a Guatemalan restaurant sounded like the closest I would ever come to a tropical treasure hunt. Plus, it was more than that. It was about chucking the dice. It was about what it's always

16

about for me: turning the clear and monotonous present into a vague and tumultuous future. I wanted to meth hunt for the same reason I agreed to join Hector in the *sky*: I had no idea what the fuck it meant. Life ought to be a game of questions, but a normal life will drown you in answers if you let it.

Gentle Guatemalan tunes played as I walked into the dining area. Thankfully the place had speakers and not a record player because the latter would have scratched upon my entry. Every table was occupied by four or five people who stared at me like the chef had stared at me: This gringo is lost. I smiled and nodded, playing it as cool as one can when scanning the floor for a baggie of meth. *Was it even in a baggie? It could be wrapped in tinfoil or something.* I could have just asked Hector what kind of vessel the meth was in, but I opted out of it for the same reason I opted out of simply having Hector relocate his own meth: It was too easy.

A waitress placed her hand on my shoulder and stared at me. Her eyes told me everything I needed to know: *You need something. I will help.* The eyes speak a million languages. It didn't matter whether this woman's native tongue was a long-forgotten language of ancient Babylon or my very own English, we didn't need the words. I stared into her brown eyes and patted my pockets, surveying the floor as to say *I've lost something.* Most people in this scenario would have been suspicious. They'd have found someone who speaks English and asked how the fuck I could have lost something in a place I'd never even been. But I knew, because of her eyes, that she was my guardian.

17

It took me by surprise when she turned off the music and gave an announcement to the restaurant, presumably explaining that I'd misplaced something. Without any delay, the whole place turned into a search party. My solo mission turned into a coordinated and bustling meth hunt: men, women, and children in hot pursuit of amphetamines. The only thing missing was drug-sniffing dogs. People were crawling on the floor, moving plates around and shifting tables, even checking their own pockets. An old woman patted down her hair as if some narcotics might have been misplaced among her gray curls. I guess when you don't know what's been lost, it could literally be anywhere. I found myself standing there, impressed and useless, like some kind of project manager, so I joined the ranks of my comrades. This meth wasn't going to find itself.

The waitress and I focused on a small religious shrine tucked away in a corner. Under the Bible? No. Behind the Virgin Mary statuette? No. The waitress even grabbed a crucifix, held it up to her face, and checked in the crevasses between Jesus's porcelain body and the wooden cross. We left no stone unturned.

"¿Qué está pasando?" *What's going on?* It was the owner of the restaurant.

The waitress scurried over to him and explained the situation. Among her words, one stood out: *metanfetamina.* She knew what I was looking for. I glanced around the restaurant and realized everyone was nodding along with her explanation. They were all on the same page. I had already been overwhelmed with gratitude when I thought that two dozen people

18

were helping me search for an unidentified object. In realizing that they had known all along it was a meth hunt, I loved them. I loved all of them. And I prayed to the miniature Jesus that the owner was one of us.

He stared at me for a moment, then shouted back toward the lobby area. The midget chef came jogging in with a kitchen knife in hand, exhaling the final plume of a just-discarded cigarette. He and the owner exchanged whispers, then the chef gestured for me to follow him. So I trailed him into the kitchen.

"This," he said, handing me a bottle of rum.

I didn't ask questions. I drank some. But apparently it wasn't sufficient because he squinted with disappointment. Before he could say anything, I took a hefty gulp, doing my best not to wince. He looked me up and down twice, finally set down his knife, and nodded. *Did I just pass some kind of test? Was this man my father?*

He disappeared into a back room for a moment, then returned and again grabbed his knife. When I took a half-step backward, he laughed.

"No, no," he said, pulling a baggie of cocaine from his pocket. "This." He dumped a small mound onto the blade of his knife and handed it to me. I had no idea what this had to do with the meth hunt, or if this guy even knew I was on one, but I obliged. I vacuumed up the cocaine, getting a close look at the knife, and by the time I looked up the chef was out the door, hustling back into the restaurant.

When I reentered the dining area, all the patrons clapped. *Did I win something?* The chef was again

19

whispering with the owner, who nodded sternly. Suddenly the two agreed upon something, and the chef shuffled over to an unmarked door near the Jesus exhibit. In he went, the door shutting behind him. I heard footsteps, the swinging of another door. Every set of eyes in the restaurant jumped back and forth between me and that door.

The flushing of a toilet, more footsteps. The chef reemerged. He was expressionless for a moment, then grinned.

He displayed a small carrot-shaped baggie of methamphetamine, raising it above his head like he'd won an Olympic gold. Chaos erupted. Shouts of joy and victory. As the chef waddled over and handed me the baggie, the music came back on. Fifty fists started to rhythmically pound on the tables in sync with the song. I spotted Hector, beer in hand, by the entrance. He nodded and smiled, giving me a look that said *I don't know what you did, but you did it, my friend.* The waitress grabbed me by the hand and guided me to the middle of the room.

We danced.

I loved her the most.

When we got back into the car two hours later, Hector popped the air conditioning dial off the center console, removing it. Behind it was a hidden chamber big enough to fit a few grams of just about anything. He put the meth into the chamber, then snapped the AC dial back into place.

I nodded with approval.

"I may be young," he said. "But I know."

"Do you have any tinfoil?" asked Hector.

We were at my kitchen table. It was midnight.

"For the meth?" I asked.

"Yes. I want to try," he said. "Let's try."

"Eh, I feel like we should hold off," I said. "I've gotta work in the morning. You working tomorrow?"

"I will work, yes."

"So maybe we just finish off the rest of the coke. Stick with the tables. And maybe Friday we can do the meth." I held up the baggie to the light. *Maybe we should just do it.* I thought about the previous six hours, the restaurant, the beloved waitress. This meth had taken me places. Was I really the kind of person who wasn't going to return the favor?

"Yes, you are right," said Hector. "We must work."

We polished off the last of the coke and said our goodbyes. As we walked out onto the porch, I wanted to let Hector know that this night, start to finish, all of it meant something to me. It was pure uncertainty, and he'd been my guide. But I didn't have the words, English or Spanish. I could blame the language barrier, but I found myself hoping that my eyes would convey some of the infinite things I felt.

"You sure you're good to drive?"

"Yes, yes," he said, glancing around the block, left then right. "I am good to drive. I am so good to drive when you remind me where did I park."

Laughter is the same in every language. And ours was loud, undoubtedly waking up the neighbors. Hector and I laughed and laughed as we paced up and down the street looking for his car. We had no fucking idea where the thing was, and as that fact became more obvious, we laughed harder and harder.

He put his arm around my shoulder: "Brother, we are so fucked. Good fucked. The good one."

"You can crash on my couch," I said.

"No, no. We will find it. But it will take maybe a long time."

"We might need some of that meth to get us focused." I was half-joking. A feeler.

"If we don't see it soon, we will try it," he said. "Maybe we go to the beach."

"What's that bird on the back of your car again? The bumper sticker."

"Quetzal."

"El quetzal es en el cielo," I said. *The quetzal is in the sky.*

"Yes, brother. Now you are knowing."

Bluebirds

I'm not a good person. I never bullshit myself about that. I drank yesterday, I'm drinking now, and I'll drink tomorrow if I'm still breathing. Saying you're not going to drink today and then proceeding to exterminate fourteen vodka sodas at Hugh Two doesn't make you good-intentioned; it makes you full of shit. A stranger to yourself. It's far wiser to drink all the time and keep your mouth shut than it is to predict your own sobriety and end up sipping a Captain and Coke with a stranger at five fifteen in the morning. It's important that I make this clear though: I would never judge someone for ending up in the latter situation. I judge them for thinking they were better than it.

The most attractive quality one can possess is a brutal self-awareness. Fuck your compassion and your IQ, your ambition and your cheekbones. None of it means a thing if you don't know exactly who you are. And I'm not talking about who you want to be, or who you think you should be, or who you were in high school—I mean the real you. The you who's hiding beneath your dreams and tattoos and memories and mascara. You're not one ounce better or worse than that person. We live in an era when a Google search can tell us anyone's history or future plans and yet most of us don't know who the fuck is staring at the screen.

I can't sleep. Back when I'd at least try to, I could only ever accomplish a half-slumber, a delirious haze, and it required a liter of rum for dinner to get me horizontal. So I did that for a while. I'd sit at the dining-room table and patiently kill a bottle of Captain Morgan. Slow and steady. There's no use rushing to bed when your mornings involve waking up feeling like life isn't something you want to partake in, then drinking enough rum to guarantee nothing will change. Plus, the mornings mean the birds. Blue ones, with gray bellies, a white patch on their throats.

Every damn sunrise they screech away in the garden, perched on the metal bars outside my bedroom window, giddily getting their precious days started. For years, my first glimpse of the sun was a white speck glinting off blue feathers, a caustic reminder that unfortunately our solar system's source of warmth and life hadn't burned out while I was semi-consciously gasping for air with my eyes shut for six hours.

I so desperately wanted to know the species of these fucking birds so that I could hate them by their full name. But by the time I got out of bed every day they were always gone. And I needed a drink. Yes, I could have looked it up, but my hangovers were so atrocious that an internet search about avian taxonomy might as well have been one of those triathlons Kenna was always talking about doing. So I long settled for hating those fucking birds in the window.

Six months ago though, I gave up on sleep. I still take a short nap in the afternoon before going to Hugh Two, but as far as the whole try-to-get-your-eight-hours thing goes, I've completely abandoned it. It wasn't really about the sleep obviously, because I've never been able to get any. It was about the hangovers. If I sleep less than two hours at a time, I avoid them altogether. Now, I'm not some kind of fucking pioneer here. It's common knowledge that the typical sleep routine means you have to stop drinking for long enough to let the devil creep in. My problem was that I thought I needed eight hours of sleep. That's what I'd been told my whole life. But that claim is just as baseless as all the other bars people set for themselves.

This gets back to self-awareness. Stop trying to do what you think you ought to do, or live up to a standard set by someone who's never fucking met you. A mindset like this steals from you, dissolves the present, destroys your very individuality. It turns your life into a never-ending attempt to meet an arbitrary standard. And, god forbid you do accomplish some goal that you think is personal despite it being instilled in you by someone else, more often than not you'll look back on that achievement not with pride but with dissatisfaction because you've inevitably relapsed back to the real you.

What a curveball.

You've gotta figure out what works for you. And what works for me is forgoing sleep, evading hangovers, and spending my extra time drinking Captain and Cokes in the dining room.

A few months back I got around to Googling the birds. There are so many fucking birds on this planet. Tens of thousands. After an hour of scrolling, I arrived at the rather obvious conclusion that the blue birds in the window are bluebirds. I admire the biologist who decided on that name, because whomever it was had an appreciation for straightforwardness. No grand labels or wordy descriptions of beak shape. It's a fucking bird. It's blue. And I've actually come to love the bluebirds. In fact, I've learned that I never hated them at all. It was the hangovers.

These days I sit at the dining-room table as the sun rises and listen to the birds chirp away, contemplating why I ever tried to blame them for anything. Their call is wonderful, really. It's repetitive, yes—basically the same shriek over and over—but it's perfectly fitting. A bird that's blue and makes only one sound. There's no confusion about what I'm dealing with here.

I was so fucked up one night last month that I was hysterically laughing at the thought of myself as a bluebird, as one of the flock. I know who I am, just like them. What you see is what you get. I don't waste my life away trying to become someone else. I grew so enthralled by the idea that I actually started squawking back at them, then with them, every morning until Mrs. Connolly called the cops. I still chirp, just not as loud. And I'd like to think that the bluebirds consider me blood.

So that's what I'm doing this morning. Drinking and chirping. My dining-room table is oak, stained light brown, the same color as a Captain and Coke. If I spill, it blends in with the tabletop, so at this point the entire surface is a glistening sheet of goodness. If the bluebirds wanted to ice skate, this would be the place. A normal person could probably lick center ice and catch a buzz. But it's a fitting centerpiece to the house because the place is a complete disaster. The table is an altar of sorts, the eye of the storm. Since Kenna left me, I haven't had any visitors other than Pancake and Lana, so there's no one to impress but myself. And to me, the home is perfectly curated. No need to straighten up and temporarily turn into one of those people who keeps a tidy home only to end up back at this table tomorrow, being me, spilling rum and remembering that I quite liked Poppy's newspaper clippings bleeding out of every drawer and Nanna's dead house plants withering away in the sun. It's the way things are. Cleaning the place up is like putting a Band-Aid over skin cancer. This house is like me— lovable if it's all you have, but easy to walk away from. And that's the way I like it. Otherwise I'd never leave.

I used to go to happy hour at Hugh Two a couple times a week, but recently I've been going every day. Someone who doesn't know me might think that's a bad sign, that I'm headed down a dark road, but it's actually a deliberate move, something I have total control over. First of all, I go there to get ideas for the book. To be among my own. That's the primary motivation. But I also go there when I'm getting too drunk. If it's just me and the dining-room table, I drink the day away and before I know it I'm a bluebird. But if I stroll down to Hugh Two, I can't possibly drink as much as I do at home because I can't afford it. So around four o'clock I walk south along the L.A. River, through all the homeless encampments. I couldn't ask for a better walk to the bar. The hobos there set up shop for the right reason—to not see people. They know what they are and they're fine with it, unlike the flocks of hobos over on Pine who want your money, your sympathy, and a job offer that'll lift them out of the gutter for six months until they relapse and end up right back on Pine with a nicer tent and sadder sob story. If they had any awareness, they'd stop running in circles and set up along the tracks. I admire the ones who do.

The smell upon entering Hugh Two is unmistakable. It's a blend of stale urine, popcorn, and cigarettes. Not lit cigarettes, although there's plenty of those. I'm talking about the ghost of cigarettes past, that scent that gains power with every burned cancer stick, an olfactory memento of all the people who have been in here killing themselves slowly because they wanted to. Everything in the place is, to put it generously, fucked. Torn carpets that take down at least one patron a night, usually Lana. Gaping holes in the ceiling. A mirror behind the bar that's shattered from top to bottom. The only thing even remotely intact is the pool table that has a three-degree tilt and a missing seven ball. But more wonderful than the bar itself are the people it attracts.

Hugh Two is a church for the hopeless. People so lost that they feel a sense of calm when they plop down on a lopsided stool as broken as they are. To the patrons here, the mirror behind the bar makes perfect sense. They look into it and see a perfect reflection of themselves, their souls shattered into a million pieces, some parts missing, stolen by some stranger-turned-lover-turned-stranger. People come to a place like this as they are—comfortably fucked-up folks who know themselves well enough to not think they're above hanging out in a bar filled with people getting half their daily calories from the popcorn machine in the corner.

I walked in around five this afternoon and sat at the bar, in the back near the fake Christmas tree. It's been set up for years. No one seems to know exactly how long, but legend says more than a decade. All the ornaments have been stolen, replaced with beer cans, empty cigarette boxes, and a few bras. As Gigi poured me a Captain and Coke, Pancake plopped down beside me with a tray of popcorn. Half of its contents spilled over the bar into the beer lake on the floor. I could tell he had been talking to himself for a while, that the conversation he was about to have with me was one that he'd already had with his alter ego.

"You see Joseph A?" he asked, gripping the edge of the bar.

Pancake calls anyone who tries to look put together a Joseph A, like Joseph A. Bank, the suit store he's certainly never been to. I glanced around the bar but didn't see anyone other than the regulars. Pancake leaned off his stool and scanned down the bar with a squint.

"Where the fuck did this guy go?" he asked himself.

"Bathroom, genius," he responded to himself.

"Yea. He's probably in the bathroom," he said to me.

"What's the guy's deal? He say something to you?" I asked.

"Not a fucking word. But he's watching me, watching everyone. Like a fucking lifeguard. Like we need savin'. He's got it all figured out, this fucking guy, let me tell ya."

He clearly wanted to rant on, but Gigi brought over a quadruple shot of vodka. More like a half glass. Some nectar spilled over the rim as Pancake slid it toward himself, creating a suction effect, the coaster desperately clinging to the glass.

"I don't blame you, buddy," he said to the coaster before vacuuming down the liquor.

He paid Gigi in quarters, re-gripped the bar as if it was his anchor to reality, then got back to it.

"There's not a snowball's chance in hell this guy's in here because he just oh-so loves the scenery. Yea, I'm sure he just can't wait to chat it up with Penny about how she beat Hep C. We're chimps. He's at the zoo, here to look at us and feel better about himself as if he's got the answer when there are no fuckin' answers!" It took all the power his necrotic lungs had to get his statement out. He started hacking onto my hand as I went to dig into the popcorn, so I shifted my excavation efforts to the section of the tray farthest away from him.

"Smokes?"

I lit him up a cigarette.

He smoked at least a quarter of it with his first drag and was still sucking down smoke when I suggested that this Joseph A might be with the health board, here to do the annual inspection. He nodded twice at the idea and removed the cigarette from his mouth for just long enough to say, "Could be," then kept inhaling. By the time he finished his first pull, the cigarette was halfway gone. He rubbed the fallen ashes into his pants and exhaled so much smoke that I could barely see him when he said, "Fucking lifeguard either way."

The bathroom door swung open and out came Joseph A. Pancake was right—someone like this doesn't walk into Hugh Two unless they're lost, serving a warrant, or here to slap the annual C rating on the murky front window. This guy was a top-of-the-line Joseph A. Older, probably early fifties, with a cockiness about him. Button-down shirt, khaki pants, and shiny shoes. Pancake visually assaulted him as he passed us, but the guy didn't give us the time of day. It wasn't until he took a seat in the stool closest to the door, presumably to have the best vantage point, that he glanced our way and gave us a nod of the head.

"Lifeguard motherfucker," said Pancake.

"Thinks he's hot shit," he responded to himself.

"Not after we get through with him," he tacked on.

"You gunna fuck him up?" I asked.

"Oh yea. We're gunna give him his," he said.

Pancake crammed a fistful of popcorn into his mouth like an athlete fueling up for a big game.

"We as in you and me?" I asked.

"Me and Lana. I'm gunna go wake her up out at the Beauty," he said with fiery sarcasm. "Me and you, you fuck. Who the fuck you think I mean by we?"

"Oh, I don't know. I thought you meant...you," I said.

"Oh, like I'm some loony fuck? What, are you gunna go lifeguard on me too? You here to save me from me, myself, and I, you cake-eating fuck?!" he shouted, waving his hands, conducting an invisible orchestra. No one thought anything of it, because it was Pancake, but Joseph A was curiously watching us.

"Pancake, stop, okay? I'm with you here. You think I like this fucking guy?" I almost wanted to tell him that I'm not so stable myself. There was the shed and my dinners with ghosts and the bluebirds.

"I know that. I know, okay? I just—" He clutched the bar, gathering his thoughts. "I hate it when these fuckers come in here and expect us to just do our usual shit while they sit up on their fucking soap boxes. And then what? We've gotta let 'em walk on outta here without smacking 'em with the truth? He's no fucking Ghandi, even if he thinks he is with that shirt and his shoes and the whole way he's doing things." Pancake leaned back in his chair and whistled at Joseph A. "Suck a dick, Joey-boy!"

"Pancake, chill out," I said, grabbing him by the shoulder. I was on probation, so a bar fight against a guy who seemed like he had the money to sue the fuck out of us was definitely unwise. For Pancake it didn't matter. He ends up in jail once every couple of months for drugs or trespassing, but they always seem to just let him go. I honestly don't understand how he never does real time. But the better half of me knew that people like us, if we stuck around late enough into the night, wouldn't be able to help ourselves. The drinks would win.

"You got any beans?" I asked. "Let's eat something."

"I'm beanless Joe Jackson," he said.

"Okay, well we'll get some more popcorn. I'll get Edgar to melt us some butter, with the buffalo sauce."

"The mixture."

"Yea, the good shit," I said. "And we'll shoot some pool. And we can go fuck with Lana, play some Shoe Clue. But let's slowplay it with this. No need to jump into anything right now, alright?"

Pancake muttered with dissatisfaction under his breath.

"I'll get your drinks," I said.

He muttered some more, his grunts sounding closer and closer to approval.

"Double vodka," I said to Gigi.

"Triple," said Pancake.

"And if the guy's still here at closing, we'll fuck him up," I said.

"Rain," said Pancake.

The popcorn machine has a consistent digestive cycle. You feed it kernels, it cooks them, the popcorn is eaten, then the machine begs for more. You can hear its emptiness before you smell it. It hisses and whines for about ten minutes, then starts to cook itself, burning away at the buttery residue and reject kernels. I'm pretty sure a normal machine would have a sensor and automatically stop cooking, but that would be a real shame. The scent of popcorn-machine autophagy is a Hugh Two staple, an incense you can't find anywhere else. And it was mighty strong tonight. We'd finished off the last of the popcorn around midnight.

It was three thirty in the morning. By my count, we'd played twenty-six games of pool, with me winning twenty-three of them. These are misleading statistics though. On most occasions, Pancake and I are very evenly matched. From a talent perspective, he is light-years ahead of me. The guy taught me everything I know about pool, and at times he's downright masterful. When I first met him, he told me he lived above a pool hall in San Pedro for a few years. It wasn't until I went there with him that I realized he meant this literally. It was a one-story building, and he lived on the roof. Anyway, sessions like these, when I'm able to dominate him, happen for two possible reasons, both of which applied on this night.

Reason one: Pancake's minds become obsessed with something else. Currently, the flavor of the night was our looming confrontation with Joseph A. For a guy with two personalities, Pancake can't multitask for shit. It's one of his finest qualities—pure integrity. He can't speak passionately about something without marrying his words to action. It's why he waves his arms when he gets fired up. He can't fake it. He's allergic to bullshit. So the twenty-six games of pool were the bullshit, the traffic jam en route to the main event against Joseph A. Pancake is his own Department of Justice. He makes the laws, swings the gavel, and doles out the floggings. But if he decrees something, any temporal gap between the proclamation itself and the carrying out of necessary action burns his soul.

Reason two was a simpler one—he went out to the Beauty between games two and three to smoke meth. He usually doesn't announce it when he heads out for a blast, but you can smell it. The meth smell is like the popcorn machine scent—unmistakable. Then he'll come back in, stop at the threshold of the back door, surveying his kingdom, and say, "Rain." You might think the uppers would help his focus, but no. It transforms his game into a rapid-fire form of pinball. He spends no time lining it up, zero strategy, and slams the ball 100 mph. The more destruction he can cause, the better. Walking entropy. And he performs what I call his meth stroke, parlaying every single shot into an air guitar solo with the pool cue.

"Kaboom-ba!" he shouted, smashing a shot wide.

I stepped up and sunk the eight ball, but Pancake wasn't even looking. He was busy strumming out the final chords of *Kashmir* by Led Zeppelin. He dropped to his knees as the song came to a close and glared at Joseph A's back.

"Hasselhoff!" he yelled. "Where's big-tit Pam?!"

"Where the fuck is it?!" screamed Lana, stumbling in the back door and stealing Pancake's attention.

"You check your pockets?" asked Pancake.

Lana slapped him full force in the face. Solid contact.

"Holy marlin," said Pancake.

"That one happened," he added.

Lana scurried over to me: "Where is it?"

"Why don't you just grab a drink, Lana? It'll help you find it," I said.

"Fuck you," she said, threatening to slap me. "Both of you can suck a fuck. Suck a dick. Suck a dick is what I meant, but you're both fucks too and you know it."

Lana stomped around the bar and foraged for her missing left shoe. Always the left one. She checked all the usual stash spots: under the bathroom sink, inside the popcorn machine, hanging from a sideview mirror out front, beneath the claw machine. One time we actually hung it like an ornament from the Christmas tree and it was there for three days until Penny accidentally ratted us out.

"You sure you had one on that foot tonight?" asked Pancake at one point. Did he not remember us going out to the Beauty earlier and stealing her shoe while she was nodding out? I genuinely couldn't tell if he was kidding. He even seemed concerned, like he might join the search.

Lana ended up storming out after ten minutes, making this one of the finest games of Shoe Clue I've ever witnessed. We had gone entirely against our usual pattern and hid her shoe in plain sight, right on the bar where she normally sits, next to the QuickDraw machine. Had she eventually sat back down at the bar and had a drink, as I'd suggested, she may have gotten a good laugh with us. That's how it goes, usually. None of the regulars can get too angry at each other. Everyone fucks up someone else's day at some point. Plus, Pancake and Lana share a tent, and I'm pretty sure he loves her. He'll get the shoe back to her eventually.

"You two want anything before I close up?" asked Gigi.

"We want the world, Gigi-baby!" shouted Pancake.

"Two double vodkas," he followed up.

I held up my pointer finger. She knows.

"It's the time," said Pancake. He nodded his head toward Joseph A, who'd been quietly observing us all night. Pancake had been spot on. We were zoo animals to this man. He'd ordered a dozen Sprites, not one ounce of alcohol. He was the type to think that he's doing it right, that he's not just like us underneath his fucking button-down and hair gel. At one point he even walked over to the popcorn machine just to stare at it. It was as though this fucking guy just wanted a close enough look to solidify to himself that he would never in his life eat out of anything so filthy. That was the turning point for me. I switched from hoping he would leave to praying he'd be around for last call.

"Penny, *Hells Bells*, my dear," said Pancake.

Penny's stool next to the jukebox is a blessing and a curse. She's on music duty. *Hells Bells* is Pancake's big-moment song. There's something about it that rattles the whole bar, shaking a gentle plaster and asbestos mist from the ceiling. I think it's the drums.

"Fuck this guy," I said, glaring at Joseph A. By this point, I think he sensed the animosity. Pancake had been screaming random shit at him all night and now we were both eyeing him like wolves, strung out on slow-cooked hatred and liquor. And some meth. I didn't think it was possible to be nervous this late in the night, but I was.

"I'm gunna go to the bathroom," I said.

"Don't you try to Irish," said Pancake.

"I just have to piss," I said. "Don't you worry."

"Smoke," he said.

I lit him up a smoke, then headed into the bathroom as *Hells Bells* came on. I didn't really have to piss. I just wanted some time with the sink. When normal people talk about meditation or exercise or being in the zone, I think of this sink. Standing in here alone, watching it, this is my now. A steady drip. Broken but constant. Drip, drip, drip. It's a metronome to degeneracy, a pacemaker for the heartless. I am where I was made to be, doing what I ought to do. This guy probably found Hugh Two on Google and decided to stop in for a while to reassure himself that, in his bullshit universe, there are good people and bad people, and he's one of the good ones. But a good person doesn't exactly get into a bar fight at four in the morning, and that's what he was about to do. We were going to make him.

I didn't have to say anything to Pancake when I walked out of the bathroom. He met me in stride. When we stopped about six feet away from Joseph A, he slowly rotated his stool to face us. Seated, but facing us. And he had this smug look on his face as if this whole thing wasn't a big deal, like he was going to diffuse the situation with some wise words and explain to us how things were going to go.

"You didn't want any popcorn?" I asked.

"All out of kernels," he said.

"We would have had Gigi throw some more in there for you if we knew you were going to sit and watch us all night like this was the fucking movies," I said, having planned that line during my personal pep talk in the bathroom.

"I'm not watching anything," said Joseph A.

"Fucking lifeguard!" shouted Pancake. "Where's your binoculars?!"

"Will you guys cut it out?" said Gigi.

Pancake grabbed Lana's shoe off the bar, firing it at Joseph A, but it missed high, breaking one of the window panels on the front door. The guy got to his feet, maintaining his arrogant poise.

"What seems to be the problem?" asked Joseph A.

"Hasselhoff!" Pancake charged full speed.

Joseph A didn't so much shove him as simply move out of the way, allowing Pancake's own inertia to send him headfirst into the claw machine. He was immediately out cold, his body limp. I remember thinking that, even though he was unconscious, you could tell he was supremely fucked up by the way his body was impossibly contorted, with his elbow bending the wrong way. He was either double-jointed or blacked out, and I'd never heard Pancake boast about his flexibility. He also must have smashed his head directly on the claw machine's START button because it started playing its happy, hopeful little jingle. The metal claw lifted into position.

"I'll have to put in a little more effort with you, I'm guessing. But it'll be the same deal," said Joseph A. "I'll lay you down right next to your friend here while we wait for the cops."

"Go fuck yourself," I said.

"Anything else?"

I glanced at Gigi, the voice of reason. She shook her head.

The adrenaline had let some reality settle in. I was thirty Captain and Cokes deep and my comrade was a schizophrenic homeless guy who had just knocked himself out on a claw machine. The saddest part is, in that moment, I didn't regret the drinking or the animosity or anything other than not spending that particular evening at the dining-room table, spilling rum, imagining that Nanna and Poppy were in the kitchen cooking lasagna.

A few months ago I actually put a lasagna in the microwave just to fill the house with that smell again, to make it more real. But I passed out and almost burned the fucking house down.

Good Catholics

Glass #1.

I stared at the fire trying to figure out what was wrong with it. I knew it was artificial, but it looked real enough; an agnostic bystander might not even notice that it was gas-powered. But something was indeed strange about it. Something beyond appearance. Or below it, I should say.

I surveyed the rest of the house to mentally inventory all of the fine things Jill and Alfonso had purchased in the year since I'd been here. I counted five cameras—three for security; one to monitor Penny, their golden retriever; and another, the most expensive, for Jill's half-hearted photography endeavors. How perverse for a camera, a device that has no purpose beyond capturing memories, to just sit there unloved because its owners are wealthy enough to let it collect dust.

Jill and Alfonso love their *things*. What they have is who they are. The seventy-inch flat-screen is Alfonso's soul. The Viking stove cranking away in the kitchen— that's Jill's beating heart. To not have these things, to get rid of the three extra cars or Hayden's iPad, would be a desecration; grounds for immediate excommunication from the American religion of possession. That's how a lot of these Long Island suburbs work. For miles in each direction, everyone is buying and buying, having and having; and, so long as they don't make a wrong turn, such is normalcy. To possess little is barbarism.

"Quite the beard," said my sister as she descended the stairs. I waved.

She looked even less human than the last time I'd seen her. Strata upon strata of makeup, her face ripe for a geological study, dyed reddish-brown hair, and the realest-looking fake breasts you've ever seen. Whoever did Jill's plastic surgery was a maestro, a prophet of deception. If I hadn't known her previous chest, I wouldn't have batted an eye.

I wanted to make a disparaging comment; but, despite being counterfeit, the mystical pair are objectively fantastic, no less under the spell of gravity than the lay population. These plastic surgeons are as good as priests; oracles of a suburban crusade. Conversion by scalpel. A homily can brighten your day. A new nose can change your life.

"Where's the Fonz?" I asked.

"Please don't call him that. He'll be down in a minute."

"Tell him to take his time."

"Don't start, please."

"I've never started anything, Jill."

"Highly debatable."

"Is it? I mean, not with him. I—"

"Just drop it, okay?"

"Yea, no, it's not a big deal. I'm just impressed, you know? In the past he at least waited until I was actually here to hate me, but this time he managed to do it in advance. It's commendable, really. When you're as shitty as him, some people can get complacent. He's actively trying to evolve and step up his game. It's good to see that, you know?"

"Luke, stop," said Jill.

Alfonso emerged atop the stairs. Freshly waxed eyebrows and a hairline that seemed to have crept slightly south since last year. He is Jay Gatsby without the mystery. A douchebag.

"Luke," he said.

"Lookin' good, Fonz," I replied. I finished off my wine and headed out the front door.

Glass #2.

The Nativity set on the lawn was obnoxious but not out of place. Half of the town had these glowing monstrosities in their front yards, each family trying to outdo not only their neighbors but themselves from years prior. I noticed Jill and Fonz even added a fourth Magi. So much for the Three Wise Men. They were willing to disregard a few thousand years of tradition if it meant *more*.

I sat there smoking a cigarette wondering who the first person was to construct a Nativity set built beyond scale. A life-size baby Jesus wasn't enough around

43

here. He had to be at least six foot three if Jill and Fonz wanted to avoid being shamed by the rest of the congregation. The self-satire was delightful. Christmas is one of the yearly opportunities for these people to convince themselves their religion is not possession but Catholicism, yet their Nativity sets beam with American hyper-indulgence. Hundreds of baby Jesuses, their mangers encrusted with gold, pitted against each other in yet another manifestation of the suburban crusade against moderation.

I chuckled to myself when I realized that, despite the grandeur, some sacrifices were made in the name of practicality; the camels, if they had been built to the same absurd scale as the infant-yet-giant Christ, would be staring into Jill and Fonz's second-floor windows. This would, of course, overshadow the importance of the Savior and, more crucially, make their house look insignificant, which would be a dual sacrilege, a betrayal of two lords at once.

Aunt Beverly and Uncle Javier pulled up in their beat-up minivan, their three young children scampering up the driveway and shouting with awe at the Nativity set. One of them tried to climb the fence, but Javier snatched him up on his way toward the house. I tossed my cigarette butt at the feet of the Virgin Mary.

"There he is," said Javier.

"Lukey-baby," said his wife.

We exchanged hugs and hellos and ridiculed the Nativity set. Javier suggested that it might be bigger than his actual house. This was so close to accurate that not laughing would have been unnatural, so we did. It was a relief to have some comrades.

Bev and Javier are the good type of Catholic. They're kind, generous, and never go to church. Because of this they know what not to believe. Catholicism is a fine religion if you know which parts to ignore. When your older sister gifts you her 2001 Corolla, you're well aware of the broken headlight and the shoddy transmission. Faith, on the other hand, is often inherited before you know how to run diagnostics. And most never do. Permanently broken gods but fixable cars.

The front door swung open. It was Jill and Fonz's son Hayden, a kindergartner. He didn't choose to enlist with the dark side, so I offered him a high-five. He hesitated, probably because Fonz corrupted him with some propaganda, but he eventually gave in, slapping my hand with fabricated enthusiasm.

"Nice watch," I said in reference to his Apple Watch. "What does it do?"

"Everything," he replied.

Glass #3.

I sat on the couch by the fire for an hour and watched as Jill and Fonz greeted the rest of the arriving family members. Based on my count, the crowd was split almost perfectly down the middle: half good Catholics, half bad Catholics. This was, of course, mere estimation. Most of my relatives are strangers to me. They show face once or twice a year and pretend to have their lives in order, which is always a red flag. Any person who shows no signs of existential crisis has either a knack for deception or a level of intelligence low enough to be a bad Catholic. In this sense, as it pertained to the looming confrontation, the distinction mattered. I prefer liars to idiots.

Uncle Pat and Aunt Kelly are firmly in the enemy camp. They, like Alfonso, attend church, consider the Bible a blueprint, and boast a deplorably unshakable faith. But, fortunately, they're poor, so at least they only live by one lie. Their poverty makes them ineligible for *things*-and-Jesus Manichaeism.

And then there's Uncle John. If he believes in anything, it's whiskey, so his loyalties are unpredictable and based mainly on his Blood Alcohol Content. Whichever side of the argument keeps the drinks flowing, he takes.

I was so deep in my preparations that I hadn't noticed Penny beside me. I gave her a rub on the back and suddenly the air smelled lovely. She must have just been groomed at one of those $500-per-day doggie spas built exclusively for people who complain about high taxes but spend $20,000 annually on an animal that would be happier in the gutter. If Penny was forced to live in the wild, she'd be done for. Any predator would pick up her scent from ten miles away and, once in range, follow the radiant glare off her coat. But I decided that Penny never wanted any of this. She was a victim of circumstance. And in setting up shop next to me, she'd made a choice—she was on my side.

Dogs don't deceive. Plus, they're too instinctual to fall for some of the shit my family has fallen for.

I spotted my cousins Laura and Phil, laughing their asses off as they walked up the driveway. It brought a smile to my face because they are brethren. I knew their cackling must have stemmed from the enormous baby Jesus or their hatred of Fonz. Get your insults out among comrades before you walk in the door, then unload again with even more venom when you leave with a buzz and fresh ammunition. Such is the practical solution to minor family feuds. If people aired out every complaint, there'd be no semblance of kinship and no time to eat. But the real pressing issues are governed by an alternative code. The more fiery a disagreement, the higher the probability it will come out at an annual family celebration. And this isn't some drunken digression from protocol. It is necessary. Better to have an annual firefight than an eternal cold war.

Laura and Phil said hi to everyone and joined me by the phony fire. We agreed we didn't mind the artificiality of it because its warmth was real.

"You guys pay your respects outside?" I asked.

"Of course," said Laura. "I'm just shocked they let the Magi into the neighborhood."

"Being colored folks and all," added Phil.

"Well they couldn't miss seeing the birth of a 220-pound baby," I said.

"Yea. Puberty got to the Lord pretty early," said Laura.

47

"If the whole Messiah shit doesn't pan out, the kid's got NFL potential," Phil said.

We laughed up a storm. I knew they were already aware of my situation with Fonz, so it required no words. They are good Catholics. They haven't been to church in a decade.

Glass #4.

I chugged a sizable glass of the sacrament in the bathroom to loosen my nerves. Some people frown upon drinking as a route to courage, but I've never agreed with that. There's a sweet spot of intoxication in which we become more of ourselves. The line is, of course, dangerously thin, and overconsumption can sometimes awaken an awful past version of us, a reemergence of a person once thought left behind. It's a kind of undesired Resurrection; a miracle in the wrong direction. That's always the game we play with alcohol. It's a process of easing inward just enough to not fall off the cliff.

I spotted a bottle of organic shampoo, the plastic seal still intact, in the shower. The same bottle was in the same spot last year. My sister has made it a point to buy organic, sustainable products. An honorable endeavor. But since she married Fonz, that goal has become murky. How good for the planet can it be to buy a sustainable product that you never use? She has been desperately clinging to a faith incompatible with the cult of having. It's acceptable to worship multiple gods, so long as you accept that each additional deity steals

48

from all the others. Big baby Jesus wouldn't be so big if they needed room for a menorah.

Glass #5.

I was sitting at the end of the table next to Laura and Phil, with Beverly and Javier across from us. All of the kids were to my left, in the central part of the table, separating us bad folks from the pious ones at the other end. This wasn't orchestrated but was how it always turned out.

The first half of the meal was rather peaceful, with each faction chatting among themselves. At one point, my sister glanced our way and smiled a real smile as though she longed to be at our end of the table. I told myself that the former version of herself, the one who agreed with me, was still in there somewhere beneath the eye shadow and perfect C-cups. This made me think of her more as a prisoner of war than an enemy. As I considered firing the first shots, Hayden, God bless his soul, fired them for me.

"Luke," he said.

"Yea?"

"Where's Alex?" he asked. Jill and Fonz exchanged a worried glance.

"Your dad said he wasn't allowed to come," I said.

"Why not?" asked Hayden.

"Because I'm gay."

"Luke, please," said my sister.

"Your dad doesn't like gay people, so he didn't want Alex to come," I said.

"Why?" asked Hayden.

"That's a good question," I said.

Hayden looked at his dad, who laughed quietly. For a moment I thought it was nervousness, an attempt to chuckle away his anxiety. But just before he opened his mouth, I realized the laugh was genuine, that he found the question so obvious as to be absurd.

"It's not natural, Hayden," Fonz said.

"You don't strike me as a fan of natural," I said.

Pristine silence, the kind that can't be found unless it has a history.

Everyone, including Fonz, knew that was the end of it. A hundred insults in a single sentence. But the victory felt hollow, for I had planned to say so much more—to tear down the house with insults, to burn any bridge that even sniffed of excess or bigotry. But it turned into my own kind of Cuban Missile Crisis—I had been prepared for a nuclear war, for ammunition to be fired until only one of us was standing. All of that turned out to be unnecessary. Blind devotion leaves many cracks, and I'd found a canyon.

I sipped Christ's blood and eyed the burning fire, realizing what was so strange about it.

It was silent.

No crackling or hissing, no whispers in its native tongue.

Details

I touch children. In the bad way. I'm the only one who seems to be able to laugh about it. I know it's not funny. It's not even remotely humorous. It's sick, actually. But laughing at it is the only way not to die. When someone gets terminal cancer, they don't sit around and tell themselves how serious it is all day. And if they do, they might as well get it over with and die. What's the point? If you can't laugh, die. And if you can't laugh at it, kill it.

I touched my first kid in 2005 at a local 4th of July parade. Events like these are ripe for predators because the parents get obliterated and are distracted by familiar faces. This is the neighborhood; our home. Who would possibly be touching kids?

Me, that's who.

If you're offended because I speak so facetiously about this, I apologize. I used to take my condition more seriously, more gravely than you could even imagine, but I've ended up here—laughing. It's my only choice. I don't want to die just yet.

When this started, I'd known for a while that I wanted to touch a kid. So this wasn't a crime of opportunity. I think that's how kid-touching works—You don't stumble upon a young boy in a back alley and, having never considered doing it before, touch him. It's an iceberg kind of thing. Ninety percent of the touching happens in the darkness of the mind. By the time I touched a real kid, I had touched a million imaginary ones.

And these thoughts, the horrible ones, were never the product of conscious effort. I never wanted to think these things. In fact, I spent years trying to *not* think them. I never put my heart into anything like I put it into suppressing the darkness. But the monster won. And for a long time, I thought he was me.

It all went down in a bouncy castle—an ideal location; that's why I chose it. This wasn't one of those castles with the see-through nets so parents can keep an eye on their kids. This particular fortress was built more in line with the classic feudal style—the only openings being the front gate and small windows through which you could see only a fraction of the interior, which was divided into four separate rooms. I don't know who designed it, but they didn't have the children's safety in mind. High walls provided cover, the loud hum of the air pump drowned out any noise, and the kids loved it in there, even the ones who went in alone. You don't need any friends when you're in a blow-up citadel with yellow walls and a trampoline floor.

Having a grapefruit-size malignant tumor on your pancreas is not funny. Dying of cancer though—you can spin that. Similarly, a kid getting touched in a bouncy castle—kind of funny. Especially if framed in the right light. But the details will wipe away any potential humor. That's the thing about turning darkness into laughter—you can't think about the details. If forced to recall them myself, I might as well die. So I must view my crimes from a distance, thinking only of the broader story and never the minutiae.

This has taken time, of course. I think it would be easier to entirely forget your own history than to do what I do—to repaint pure darkness as comedy by means of abstraction. But I've gotten quite good at it. One technique I use is to think of myself in the third person. This makes my life more of a story than an identity. Another strategy is to take the settings of my real crimes and plant them somewhere else, some imaginary place. Let's say I touched a kid behind a dumpster at a basketball court—which I obviously didn't actually do because getting that specific about the location would be counter to my whole agenda here, but hypothetically—I would imagine that it really happened behind a woodshed at a soccer field. I shift the location to something that I can half-imagine but can't fully place myself in. This is step one, because it allows me to step outside myself, to turn a memory into something fleeting, something that falls through my hands like sand instead of crushing my soul like a boulder. My former self becomes someone else, like I'm watching me from a drone with a foggy lens.

So yes, I touched a kid on July 4, 2005, in a bouncy castle. I won't go much deeper than that. Trust me, when this actually happened, it wasn't funny for me. It

53

was the opposite—absolute darkness. And I don't want to go back there. You can turn this sickness into humor only if you've lived with it for as long as I have. Not many patients chuckle moments after the doctor informs them they have stage IV lung cancer. I can only hope that, in time, they're able to laugh about it.

It would eventually become well-known that Martin was a pedophile. For most inmates, your background comes to light immediately, and intentionally, because your convictions are your armor. If you're in for something vicious like murder or assault, it's best to get the word out early and let everyone know you're capable of swift violence. This genre of evil— instantaneous violence—is the most valuable form of depravity on the inside. Most incarcerated are obviously capable of some form of wickedness; but the ability to, at a moment's notice, fight like an animal is the most precious commodity among the caged. Those whose methods of sin are more slow-moving and cerebral are at a distinct disadvantage. Martin began to see this dynamic, the division between categories of evil, and he knew very well which side of the equation he fell on: He was the prey.

In his early days, Martin spent time lifting weights, shadowboxing, doing thousands of push-ups in his cell at night. But he gave up when he realized it only brought him unwanted attention. Working out, Martin learned, was just another form of armor, but a weak one. Looking like you're ready for violence has little correlation with an actual readiness. Often it was those who looked least physically powerful who committed the most inconceivable bloodshed, usually by sneak attack. Martin realized that this trait—a taste for violence—was no different than generosity or creativity or humor. Some people have it in their blood, others do not.

"I beat the fucker with a pedal wrench. You know what a pedal wrench is?" said one prisoner over the lunch table.

"For fixing pedals, I assume? On a bike," responded another.

"For pedals, yea. You can use 'em on bikes, but I worked at the state fairgrounds, up in Raleigh. They had those pedal boats you take out on the lake."

"Pedal boats? Those like paddle boats?"

"Same shit, yea."

"The guy live or…?"

"Unfortunately."

Martin was never involved in these conversations, but he always listened. Eavesdropping became a passion. He made it a point to inventory the crimes of other inmates, scribbling down their atrocities in his notebook. This was his way of fighting an idea that he couldn't stop thinking about: that he was worse than all of these people. An outsider looking into the prison might see Martin quietly keeping to himself, steering clear of the fighting and mayhem, and consider him relatively good; an unlucky bystander trapped among animals. But Martin knew the truth: He was perhaps the most monstrous of them all; the vertical bars and concrete kept his sickness stowed away, hidden for only himself to see and feel and hate. So he kept writing in his notebook, day after day, line after line, hopeful that if he continued to detail the gruesome crimes of his peers he could forget about the monster within himself.

No one cares about a thing that's halfway something. If something is half bad or half good, you can simply call it what it is. Only when it moves to one extreme pole is it essential to take notice and call it what it isn't. If your life is just so amazing, so perfect, it's important to remind yourself that it's not that good. Because if you're convinced it's really so flawless, when you lose what you have, which you will, it will be downright awful. So you need to plan ahead. That's the whole game here.

So, yes, if I told you about every kid that I touched between 2005 and 2010, we would both have the same opinion: What I did is absolutely deplorable, an abomination, the worst possible thing. I would rather die. But here we are at an extreme pole; one of those situations when, if we are to protect ourselves from ourselves, it is in our best interest to call it what it isn't. And it definitely isn't funny, so that's what we'll call it.

I am not the victim here. The kids are the victims. Trust me, I agree with that. I wholeheartedly do. I see them in my nightmares every night. Their tortured eyes. Their broken souls.

Their perfect, unclothed bodies.

(I'm kidding about that last part. I was getting too close to reality, so I had to inject some humor.)

I really do see them though. And I can't escape it. If there was a way to quit sleep, I would do it. The thought of my bed brings terror because I know the horror that comes with a good night's sleep. And I can't get more than a few feet away from the bed in this cell.

I must again stress that I am not the victim, not in the traditional sense—I am a monster. The darkness. But I am, at the very least, a victim of a few things. Of bad luck, that's for sure. Of flawed genetics. Of a disease. But more than anything else, I am a victim of myself, my own beliefs. I have been a slave to the idea that I have an inescapable fate.

But not anymore.

Other than the guards and prison staff with whom he sometimes had to communicate with, Martin spoke to only two people in the six months that he'd been caged. One conversation was a brief exchange about the poor quality of the mattresses. Another involved a man asking Martin if he'd ever been to Las Cruces, New Mexico; which he hadn't. Neither of these interactions was particularly personal, and both lasted less than thirty seconds, but that didn't matter. The interactions, regardless of their content, gave Martin a rush of humanity, as if he'd found food after weeks of starvation. His mind was telling him, for his own good, that he ought to nourish his social desires. He should talk to someone, anyone. He should find a friend. He wanted to with all of his heart, but he knew that any decent conversation or friendship would lead to the inevitable question: Why are you in here?

So Martin fought the primal urge for companionship. He walked the yard alone. He always ate alone. And if another prisoner stole his food, which often happened, he would let it go without a fuss. One day, when an inmate stole a piece of bread from Martin's tray, he considered a confrontation—not for the sake of the bread or for his own pride, but because it would force him to interact with another human being. Martin thought this was possibly why overly reclusive people became either schizophrenic or violent: If the mind doesn't get human-to-human connection, it will find a way to steal it.

One way is to go crazy, to invent companions and plot lines and an imaginary social construct. But if one is not genetically susceptible to insanity, the brain will find another way to tie into the web of humanity. What better way to dive back into the human ecosystem than to shoot up a school or go on a killing spree? If a man is committed ardently enough to lonesomeness, a bullet is perhaps as close as he can get to hello. But Martin turned neither crazy nor violent. He realized that, while he wasn't born with the gift of swift violence, he was adept at sustained warfare against his most primal urges.

Around a year into his sentence, Martin sensed that things were changing. He could tell by the way other inmates looked at him that they knew his secret. If a man keeps his crimes to himself for too long, it's likely because he committed one of the unspeakable ones. He was a child molester. He knew that his own silence would eventually back him into a corner, which was his goal. He could never truly confront his own darkness, so flat-out admitting his sins wasn't an option. But more important for Martin, he wanted the punishment. He needed it.

Whatever street justice was coming his way, he deserved it. When the other inmates finally got to him, he thought, when he was turned into a sex slave or shanked in the neck or beaten to death—this was his fate. He was born a monster, did monstrous things, and ought to receive the punishment a monster was owed. For over two years, every time he took a shower or ate in the cafeteria or turned a corner, Martin waited for an attack. But retribution never came.

He had so woven this truth—that child molesters get abused in prison—into his fate that he was distraught by the possibility of it not happening. He'd long hoped that fate would give him what he truly deserved and allow him to forget his sins. Why couldn't someone just do what was right and kill him? A small piece of Martin began fearing the worst: There could be no separating himself from the monster. If he wanted to kill it, that would be the last thing he'd do.

In 2010, a child was feeling empowered, like action was his best course. Of all the children to have a fiery spirit on that particular day, I can't for the life of me understand why he had to be one of the few who I've touched. It's that bad luck again. There are a billion kids across this planet, and this one decides to be a crusader. I'll call him Henry Plummer. (No details. Remember?) Henry told his dad what I did to him. I knew his dad, we were friends, so he found the allegations outlandish. And so did I. *Me? Ridiculous! He's a damn child! He's making up stories like children do!* (I shouldn't have used exclamation marks there, because I was relaxed. I didn't scream. And if this wasn't handwritten, I would delete those.) *He's a damn child. He's making up stories like children do.* That's what I said. I was perfectly calm. And it worked! Like I said, I knew his father and he knew I was a good guy. That poor kid told his darkest truth and his own dad scoffed at it. It's so beyond terrible that I can't help but chuckle thinking back on it.

Then little Henry-who-isn't-really-Henry started telling other people—his friends, neighbors, everyone. There's nothing worse than people talking. I have spent years and years sitting with the fact that I am the darkness. The last thing I needed was everyone else knowing it. But the dominos started to fall. Henry's chatter brought other kids out of the woodwork. Accusation upon accusations. By themselves, basic accusations aren't all that bad. But what put the nail in the coffin was the same thing that I've spent years trying to blot out—the fucking details. No child, even one with the most diabolical imagination in the history of mankind, could make up the very real details these kids lived through. If a kid simply says I touched him, so what? It's my word against his, and kids tell stories. I could look back at that and laugh it off. But if a kid says you removed his pants in a dark-blue Honda Accord with the back seats folded down, closed the window screens on the back windows, and used olive oil to...

See what happened there?

The minute those damn details get involved, two things happen. One, I turn into a monster and end up in prison because the story gets too specific to take lightly, especially from a child. And two, it all becomes not funny. No one knows this more than me. None of this has ever been even remotely funny.

So I laugh at it.

For as long as he could remember, Martin had dreamed of molesting children. And he despised these visions. He avoided sleep at all costs for most of his adult life; for while he slept, the monster gained strength. But a few years into Martin's prison sentence, once he'd given up hope on receiving retribution, his dreams changed. He started to fantasize about his own death. He'd envision himself being stabbed with sharpened broom handles in the showers or strangled to death in the yard, with all of the other inmates joining in, kicking and spitting on him—because it's what he had deserved. Eventually these dreams became exactly like his dreams about children. They were horrific and inhumane and everything he wanted.

But fate never showed up. Martin realized that everything he'd been told about child molesters in prison wasn't true, at least not entirely. And this revelation destroyed his entire ideology. The inevitability of his own brutal demise was the only way he'd been able to live with himself. It was supposed to

61

be the period on the sentence of his sins. It would kill the monster. Could the world really turn a blind eye?

Martin realized what fate was telling him: He'd have to take matters into his own hands. It was his only choice. He spent years trying to live with himself, to look his monster in the eyes and call it something other than pure darkness. But he couldn't. Any honest look at his own past sent him the same message: die. So that was his plan. He began collecting textile scraps to construct a rope, hiding them in a slit in his mattress. It took countless nights of work, but eventually he tied together enough towels and kitchen rags and socks to have a sturdy rope. His time had come.

When the lights went out on a winter night, he hanged himself. As his brain approached blankness, he felt his feet graze the floor. The rope was slipping, weakening; then it snapped, dropping Martin to the floor. His head smashed against the concrete.

Martin woke up before sunrise, a pool of dried blood around his face. But he felt refreshed for the first time in twenty years. Something was different, and he sensed it. He lay there in silent contemplation for a few minutes, and then his dream came back to him. It settled into his psyche like a final piece of a puzzle— the monster had come to terms with itself. He sat up and laughed uncontrollably. It was a laughter so primal that he barely caught his breath. For the inmates in the surrounding cells, it was the first noise they'd ever heard from Martin. Some cursed and threatened him, but he didn't care. He was a caged man with a funny disease.

Unfortunately, I'm set to be released tomorrow. And I'd love to say I'm a changed man, but I'm not. Obviously, I haven't touched any kids in ten years, but that's only because there's no kids in here. Trust me, I still have my dreams. The iceberg remains. And I've often fantasized about the many prisoners in here who are on the younger side, around eighteen or nineteen. But they're never young enough for the monster.

All of this is perfectly fine as long as I'm locked up. Yes, I touched kids back in the day. And yes, I think about kids. So what? It's hilarious. But I know what's waiting for me on the other side of these concrete walls. Once I'm out there, things will become not funny very quickly. You can't laugh at the details while you're living them.

No one was there to pick Martin up. But he'd expected this. His family had disowned him, and the few friends he had in his past wished they'd never met him. Nonetheless he felt more empowered than he'd ever felt. For the first time in his life, he felt like the master of his own fate. Life wasn't something that was happening to him. It was something he could steer and manipulate and dominate. He hadn't given up on the idea of fate, but rather he saw fate as something to be crafted according to his desires.

There was a park two miles away from the hotel, and Martin decided it was the perfect location. He ate a wonderful breakfast of waffles and eggs and orange juice before calling a taxi. The driver smiled and chatted with Martin, having no inclination that a monster sat in his rearview. The man told Martin to have a nice day, and it even seemed like the two could become friends. This tickled Martin's soul, but the joy quickly ran off when he realized that, if the driver truly knew him, he would have refused to pick Martin up in the first place. He would rather Martin be dead.

As Martin entered the park gate, he was hit with a wave of what he would have previously called intuition. But his outlook had changed. It wasn't a feeling. It wasn't a hunch that something big was about to happen. It was control. Martin was about to make a choice with undeniable consequences and smack his reality in a new direction. Fate, he'd learned, wasn't something that was going to work itself out to the perfect end. If it was, he'd be dead. Instead, fate was a thing to be wrangled.

Every breath he took felt like one step closer to his objective, like he was inhaling the future. He paced across the park, pine needles crunching beneath his feet. The world seemed to be nothing more than a stage for what he knew would be his last act outside of the cage. He was playing God, harnessing that heightened sense of awareness that one cannot achieve unless a moment mattered. He reached around to his lower back and felt the gun. He'd never used one before, but today he had to.

That's when he heard them: children.

He heard and saw everything. Every adorable laugh, every shriek, every detail. The sound of friction the slides make against a child's bare skin. The rhythmic grinding of the chains on the swings. The mothers chatting among themselves, intermittently shouting to check on their children. These were the details that could quickly become the darkness if he let them. So he briefly defended against them, chuckling to himself as he unzipped his fly. But then he let the monster take the reins.

Martin masturbated on the park bench as he watched the children. He had fantasized about this very moment thousands of times in prison, but his imagination always struggled with the details. They meant everything to him. Not a single thing escaped him. And he knew none of it was funny. He was a monster. He was the opposite of light.

He zipped up his fly and headed toward the playground, enjoying one final and intimate look at the children as he passed. Across the street was an Italian deli with a $7.99 lunch special. Martin strolled in and raised the gun, pointing it at the cashier's head. The man pleaded for him not to shoot, but it didn't matter. The bullet tore through a tall stack of to-go containers.

"Call the police," said Martin.

I meant to miss, of course.

21D

I watched as the flight attendant made her way down the aisle with the drink cart. She was an overweight blonde woman with an infectious smile, taking her sweet-ass time. Row by row. Every stop she made was salt in a wound I couldn't locate. The surface-level reason I took issue with her leisurely pace was obvious—I wanted a drink. Or six. I have always hated airplanes. But my irritation wasn't simply about the slow-passing time. It was something more than that. I found myself irked, in some way I could not understand, by her every utterance. Nothing about the words themselves bothered me though, as she was perfectly courteous, dishing out pleasantries but not overdoing it. A respectable woman. I did my best to set aside my obscure animus as she docked the cart just past me in the aisle.

"Anything to drink, darling?" she asked, her voluptuous left hip nestled against my left shoulder. This triggered a strange indecisiveness, an emotional tug-of-war. I liked her hip. And I liked what she was saying, because I really did need a drink. But I hated that she was speaking. Her words, agreeable as they may have been, hurt some part of me I wasn't acquainted with.

"Two rum and ginger ales," I said.

"Are they both for you?"

"Yea, why? Is there a one-drink-at-a-time rule or something?" I was almost hoping she would say *yes* and provide me with a tangible reason for my germinating hostility. Such a response would have pegged it as something closer to intuition.

"Sort of, yea," she said. "But one's for him, right?"

She winked, gesturing to the empty middle seat beside me, and began preparing my drinks. Here was a lovely woman breaking the rules on my behalf, yet I hated her. The backwardness of it sent a shudder of anxiety up my spine, my jaw clamping shut, my temples twitching. I wasn't so much scared that things didn't make sense. I was horrified that they soon would, that my reality would be obliterated in the confines of this cabin.

TV. The TV in the headrest. Music. Hotel California. Noise-cancelling. Low battery. Bacon and—

"Thank you," I said. It was not the time to run.

I couldn't suppress the feeling that this flight attendant was a rum-bearing angel sent at thirty thousand feet to save me from my invisible complexes. Half of me wanted to turn back, to numb myself with culture and forget about her; but the other half, the half that sought to expose myself, knew that I would be an enemy of my own evolution if I tried to evade the impending news. I stared at her and basked in the hatred, hoping it would come to an elucidating boil. By the time she set down my drinks, I was swimming in unexplainable rage. I did, however, manage to thank her, as she did a more-than-stellar job. I made clear that I would be ringing the call button for more drinks soon. Very soon.

I downed my first drink in two gulps, an unruly ice cube escaping onto my lap. As I swept it onto the floor, the man in the window seat, a kind soul in his fifties, noticed me do it. He did not, in any discernible way, judge me. He simply witnessed the ice cube disposal, presumably by accident, and passed no verdict. I stared into his impartial eyes. They offered me nothing—no criticism, no assessment, nothing worthy of response. He returned his gaze to his book, which happened to be *Dune*, my favorite book of all time. But despite his undeniable innocence and our unspoken literary kinship, the same feeling—the one I had about the flight attendant—gurgled in my depths. A veiled hatred.

The whole situation so reeked of impending self-realization that I downed my second drink in a swift opening of the throat. Turbulence shook the plane. Swift inhalations. The collective tensing of a few hundred abdomens. I thought for a childish second that the scenario was a fitting backdrop for my stormy mind, setting the stage for my looming shift in consciousness; but the self-centeredness of this naive thought only pushed me further toward dread. I was teetering on hysteria. It had begun.

I saw every single face as I paced toward the back of the plane. No passenger escaped my unjustified resentment. I even locked eyes with an infant, an Asian girl swaddled in her mother's arms, and detested her. Undeniable. Once your mind accepts the unrelenting approach of revelation, it acquiesces, magnifying your complexes and exposing the caverns of your psyche. But existential torment requires translation, and I had not the slightest idea what I was trying to tell myself. I swung open the bathroom door, which functioned like every other airplane bathroom door I'd ever encountered.

"Sir, the seat belt light is on," said the flight attendant. Scathing words.

"Sorry," I replied, keeping my head down as I shut the door and locked it, hoping that upon emergence I would be an upgraded man who had successfully figured out why he hates that which ought not be hated.

Dim yellow light. Industrial chemicals. Alone. I flipped down the toilet cover and took a seat. My fear subsided fractionally, so I took the low-hanging fruit, deeming this revelation of mine a rather basic one—I prefer solitude. Of course. That was it. I despise planes because they are cages for the plenty. And these people were my enemies because they were a hindrance to my isolation. Pure logic. Yes, sometimes the simplest of self-truths are forgotten because of their glaring fundamentality. Revelations are often a reversion, the relearning of that which we already knew. My world, therefore, would not be pulverized and made entirely anew, but rather reassembled into a previous form that had been haphazardly set aside. I nodded repeatedly as though every rise and fall of my head further verified the claim.

Crossword puzzle. A movie, yea. Meeting with Kent. Tuesday. Graham's wedding. Cleveland. July 21—

My reaching for a tissue, the robotic yanking of a Kleenex from a stack of thousands, a motion performed by hundreds of people per flight, brought the hatred back in a roaring instant. The fire had never left. It only needed oxygen. I became acutely aware of my own deception, my internal propaganda—an act of self-preservation, really; a skirmish between myself and what I would become. One need not look beyond the self for proof of Darwinism. I had clubbed and dragged the impending me down into the lightless cavities of my psyche in the hopes that he'd stay put, but he again escaped to demand a proper examination. And he was stronger now. Survival of the fittest. I blew my nose with trembling hands and slipped the tissue through the mechanical flap of the trash bin. The movement of that flap, its predestined clanking back into position, fanned the flames. Hatred. More and more evidence was being strewn across the table. In every glance lurked messages from the me that was dying to take my place.

"Can I get two more rum and ginger ales, please?" I said as I exited the bathroom.

"You're having a good time, huh?" said the flight attendant.

"We're having a good time," I said. "Me and the guy next to me. In the middle seat."

"Oh yea," she said. "He seems like a good guy. A tad shy though. Really keeps to himself."

She grinned and got to work. This woman, to my rational mind, was nothing short of a saint. I even felt a subtle sexual attraction to her. Nonetheless: hate. And it would continue until I figured out why. Irrationality, if pursued properly, can be the mother of self-discovery. Oftentimes the road that makes the least sense leads one to himself, so long as he gets off at the right exit.

I scanned the backs of all the passengers' heads as I hurried back to my seat. I couldn't even see their faces, but I abhorred them all. I retook my assigned seat and was met by my black reflection on the headrest TV. Panic. A lifetime's fear in a glance. That was the authentic me, the person within myself crying for recognition. He was what I hated. This enigmatic hostility, I realized, was a loathing of something deep within me. I readjusted in my seat as if there was some position that would end the war. I twisted open the overhead vent, a cool breeze kissing my forehead.

Laptop. TED Talk, maybe. No wi-fi. Mom's birthday. More rum. Neurologist. Uber. Trader Joe's dark—

"Two rum and ginger ales for you, gentlemen," said the stewardess as she set down my drinks and disappeared before I could properly dislike her. The kind soul by the window glanced my way with confusion, thinking perhaps one of the drinks was for him, so I stared back at him with unflinching animosity, hoping to track my hatred for him to its source in the trenches of my soul. After a few seconds, he looked away. It felt like something out of the movies, when they try to trace the villain's phone call but he hangs up before his location is pinpointed. I threw one of my drinks down the hatch, chewing a few ice cubes as I waited for the next signs. My eyes jumped to my seat number.

21D

An ocean of despair. Whirring engines. An emotional déjà vu…

I was around nine or ten years old, flying from Maryland to New York. I gripped the airplane armrests. Images, thousands upon thousands of pictures in the span of seconds. Blue seats. A pack of Juicy Fruit. Passengers, passengers, passengers. White men in black suits. Vomit in a toilet. An old, haggard pilot. Phil. James. My mother's worried face. Her hand on my back. Gates and terminals and planes upon planes. Prisons of the sky. Dunkin' Donuts. A subway map of Manhattan. Swarms of humans riding the—

Turbulence. The fuselage rattled. A gasp from 22F. A chorus of seat belts clicked. It was an old story on a new page—partly new. But the feeling of elusive hatred—I had lived it already; a crippling self-hatred of unknown origins, tucked away in the undercarriage of my soul. I never hated planes, or the passengers. It was just the survivalist lie I used to hide from myself.

My eyes traced the overhead bins that neatly lined the ceiling, one after the other. Precision. The brainchild of blueprints. The whole aircraft was a repetition of itself, and of another of its kind, a lesson in uniformity. Seat after seat, armrest after armrest, plane after plane. Symmetry. A submissive machine that operated as it was designed to operate. I hated all of it. Every plane, seat, tray table, window, airport, and passenger. I detested everything and everyone within reach of my imagination; I had to if I wanted to kill off the imposter.

More turbulence jolted my head forward against the headrest. I clutched my drink, managing to consume the entire thing amid the turmoil, rum dripping off my chin in the madness. As the plane settled, the rumbling of the cabin becoming the low hum of engines, I glanced to the kind soul by the window, 21F, and my hate for him dissolved. A complete one-eighty. I turned the gun on myself.

My hostility materialized as fully explainable self-loathing. Truth splattered onto the windshield of my consciousness. These passengers were me. I hated them because I was inarguably one and all of them, an exact copy. Planes, where human beings are assigned a number, fed identical meals, and rightfully considered replicas of each other. I evaporated. Individuality is a cozy lie we tell ourselves, a blind attempt to convince ourselves that this airplane is any different from the planet below, a rock tearing through space carrying billions of primates doing everything in their power to ensure their own selfhood. Sadness.

21D

It glowed with spectacular homogeneity.

JFK. Chipotle. Won't be open. Two hours. Haircut. Mark's backyard. LeBron Ja—

I dinged the flight attendant bell. The plane banked right, some Midwestern city shining below, its gridded streets stacked one on top of the other. I was one of those streets, or streetlights, or light bulbs. Or just a human being. I had long considered revelations to be inherently good and natural, a progression toward what truly is. But I longed to return to my previous illusion—to carry a sliver of mysterious hate for others is a small price to pay for permission to believe you're not a statistic. I should have stayed on the ground, for this metamorphosis was not something I would have chased had I known the outside of the cocoon would destroy me.

"Let me guess. Two more?" asked the stewardess to the man in the seat ahead of me. Kick me while I'm down. After a short confusion, she realized she had the wrong seat.

"Sorry. Can't see anything on these red-eyes," she said, toggling off the call button.

"No worries," I said.

"Two more?"

"Three," I said, gesturing to the kind soul by the window. 21F smiled and nodded, accepting my peace offering to end a battle he never knew was waging. As the stewardess vanished into the darkness to fetch the drinks, I felt a sense of calm that she, the talking one, was gone. Yet I could hear the faint sound of her voice near the back of the plane. I couldn't make out the words, but even that distant, indecipherable chatter crippled me. The war continued.

A TV screen three rows up, being watched by 18C, showed an interview with a NASCAR driver, babbling away. The movement of his mouth brought about an equal level of disdain, a shifty jealousy; a dissatisfaction with the fact that this plane was a place where I had to keep my mouth shut. I considered the possibility that speaking, the formation of unique words and sentences, was a route to individuality. Young hope. Sunshine. That must be why the flight attendant's speech was so damaging to me. She was, in this floating jail, the only one free to distinguish herself from the rest of us by means of unrestricted discourse. I nodded my proposal into plausibility.

Hibachi with Christie. Call of Duty. Mom's b-day, got that. Pita chips. Saturday night at—

"Good to see you're making friends," the flight attendant said as she arrived with our booze.

"With everyone but myself," I said, prompting a genuine chuckle from her as she gathered the trash from my previous drinks.

A profound satisfaction crept in as I weighed the idea that what I'd just said, in the context that I'd said it, had never been said before. Special. Stand-alone. A flurry of coughs from 19C.

My rational mind countered, running numbers in my head, and arrived at the fact that, among the billions and billions of people who have lived, someone had almost certainly said something exactly like what I just found to be so sharp-witted and original. Speaking was merely my heavy artillery, the best strategy I had in the struggle to manipulate myself into thinking I was not everyone else and they were not me.

I caught myself red-handed. I sat aboard a flying *Beagle*. What I had thought was another signal from the undiscovered future me was really a last-ditch effort by what remained of the fraud, a clinging to the possibility of differentiation. Hopelessness. Deletion. Two apes became one. I disappeared, expanded. I was nowhere and everywhere at the same time. Horizontal dominos. Blankness.

"You three behave," said the stewardess as she took off. They were benign words; air.

21F said what anyone in his shoes would have said: "Thanks for the drink."

I tapped my cup with his and initiated a conversation. Our dialogue started slowly, as most do, but it escalated into an alcohol-fueled existential exchange.

"We're really the same, all of us," I said.

"Sort of, I suppose," said 21F. "But in many ways, we're not. I mean, look at the diversity across the globe. Every culture is different. It's—"

"But, ironically, that's fading," I said. "Globalization might seem like the bringer of diversity, like it's exposing us to cultural differences, but really it's the very force that will demolish it. It'll create a monoculture. One big capitalist world. But that's not even my point, really. My point is that when you look at other cultures and think they're different, that's an illusion. They're not. Their flags are different colors and they like soccer and they use turmeric instead of salt, but underneath all of the bullshit, they're us. Maybe that's what cultures really are. They're systems we create to feel special."

My horrific realization seemed to have melted away my creative filters. Oddly, my acceptance of my own inability to say anything unique was allowing me to fire off things that I hadn't heard before. At least not from myself. A crying baby up near row 14. Snoring from 22E.

Our drunken banter attracted others. The woman in 21C, a psychologist, and the college student in 21B joined the assembly. After a few more rounds of drinks, I opened up to my new council of friends about my recent revelation—that all human beings are the same, how our names are mere clever seat numbers. Nicely said. I insisted that we are all genetic copies of one another wasting our lives in the futile effort of evading this truth, mainly by way of speech. A clear thesis. Counterintuitively, I even enjoyed a minor satisfaction at the way I verbally packaged and delivered these ideas despite the theory itself reinforcing the fact that my hypothesis was just a reformulation of something already said by someone else. During lulls, I made sure to remind myself of this; that I was an old saga with a new face. One ape. Water vapor from the air vents. Sneezes from 19F.

When I finished making my case, my comrades sat in silence, pondering. I waited eagerly for one of them to say something. Nihilism tinged with glee. Most of me felt infallible, that I'd arrived at what is; but a fraction of me wanted to be proven wrong, to be shoved back into believing there was hope of individuality.

Ding. The seat belt light turned off. Clicks. A herd on the move. The college student in 21B was particularly rattled, and I regretted involving him. He was too young. He deserved more time living under the delusion that he wasn't just like us.

"Everything we do has been done before," I said. "It's like the bullshit they tell you about snowflakes or fingerprints. I'm not buying it. If we inventoried every fingerprint in history and every snowflake to ever fall from the sky, there would be duplicates. I guarantee it."

"That's not entirely true," said 21C. "It's mainly correct, yes. Most people will never say an original thing or create an original piece of art or music or poetry or architecture. But there are some people, a select few, who definitely do something entirely new. Albert Einstein, for instance. He discovered something fully novel, a whole new way of understanding the universe." Her delivery was confident, a sign that she'd had similar thoughts before and taken up arms against them.

78

"But the truth was there all along," I said. "It wasn't new. He just discovered something that was already there, waiting for one of us to see it. Yea, some people say math is invented, but really, it's discovered. That's what most people whose opinions are legitimate think."

"Correct," she replied, again in a tone that let me know she was well-equipped with reason. "But to discover something or create something that causes a cosmic shift in consciousness—that is original. E equals mc squared. No one in the universe, unless you're absurdly speculating that some aliens beat us to the punch, had ever thought of that. And what about someone like Copernicus? People used to think Earth was the center of the universe. He figured out it wasn't even the center of our solar system. If that's not a unique perspective, I don't know what is."

There was an announcement from the pilot, so 21C upped her volume: "I think what you're wrestling with is the fact that, because we were born into a rather advanced society, it's a lot harder to think of anything new. The cracks in reality, the mysteries, the unique stories, they're harder to come by. It was a lot easier to discover something new when people still thought death was caused by ghosts and God cooked up hurricanes. Same goes for art. The more stories or songs or paintings that pile up, the harder it is to write one that's not just a remake of one from the past. But you're wrong to assume it's impossible. It's just hard. Really hard. And Einstein was just the most extreme example. He wasn't the best case to bring up, because there are plenty of people who create new things at a smaller scale. Micro-discoveries or little advances in art or whatever. But only gifted minds can do it. There's no doubt about that. It's just very, very rare to be one of those people."

Everyone nodded her statement into truthhood. I joined them. A row of bobbing heads. 21B. 21C. 21D. 21F.

"And what I just said has definitely been said before," she chuckled as more drinks arrived. "Because I'm one hundred percent not one of those people."

Everyone but me laughed and agreed that they, too, weren't one of the chosen few. Crushing. Why would the woman who had presented this brilliant idea insist that she was not a gifted mind?

Burrito bowl. Pinto, no, closed. John Snow. Cracked screen. That new place on 14th. Home—

I surveyed the plane. The exit row, yes. Seats 17A–F. Those six seats, a tiny fraction of the hundreds of seats on board, represented the chances I had of being unique among humans. And even that was a generous estimation, a mathematical nudge of the lines in the direction of hope; the deathbed work of the terminally ill ape. Real logic indicated daunting odds. I was Darwin himself, an objective witness to the clashing species within myself. One primate. Not special. 21D.

Morning light. Window shades opened. The me of yesterday gasped for air. I thought perhaps I needed to retain some hallucination of uniqueness to survive, to continue the strife within myself; lest I lose all sense of competition and not evolve. Adaptation. The last thought I remembered thinking was that this was the most human thought I'd ever had.

Blackness. Cookies and cream. 21F. Fuck you! Vomit. 21C. 7F. Rug burn. JFK—

"21D," said the stewardess.

I opened my eyes to bright fluorescent light. Handcuffed, my back to the wall in a small white room. Rebirth. The police officer flashed me judgmental eyes as he scribbled in a notepad. Two TSA employees lingered by the door. Badge numbers. Uniforms. The AC vent. The faint rumble of sprinting planes. An infinite appliance. The world.

"Shit is outrageous. You must feel pretty good about yourself," said the officer before leaving the room, the TSA workers trailing him out. A blue flock.

The flight attendant avoided eye contact. The details escaped me, but…outrageous—that's what he called the situation. And I had done it, whatever it was. It tickled the smoldering remnants of my former self; a pulse from the dead ape—squeezing handcuffs, a throbbing brain. The Galápagos. Natural selection. Outrageous.

"Are you going to lose your job?" I asked.

"Probably. But there's plenty of other airlines."

"Sorry."

"That's alright. Happens more than you think."

The Man Who Hates Strip Clubs

"Sure you don't," said Daisy.

"I'm serious. I don't actually like 'em," said Kenny.

Daisy was on Kenny's lap. There were four other patrons in the club. You can never be too sure though, because of the darkness. Sometimes one might stare into the abyss only to spot Leonard slouched in a chair, lifting a rum and Coke to his lips.

"You think I'm lyin'," Kenny said. "But that's just 'cause you lie for a living."

"Really, Kenny? Fuck you."

"No, no, don't take it like that. It's one of the things I love about you. It's beautiful, the way you girls lie. I mean, anyone who knows anything knows not to believe a goddamn word any of you say. But if you just—"

"I should get back to work."

"Yea, 'cause there's just boatloads of money to be made right now."

"Guy by the ATM looks hopeful."

"Daisy, Daisy, Daisy—money's money, of course, but never trust a man by the ATM. Have I taught you nothing? If a man sits near the ATM, it's a hundred percent calculated. 'Cause when you look at him, you can't help but see money. It's a subconscious thing, sure, but it's there. And he knows it. He knows when you see him over there that you can't help but see dollar signs. He's fishin', that's all."

"Yea, I'm sure it has nothing to do with the fact that that's the first chair you see when you walk in," said Daisy.

"Now how much sense does that make, Dee?"

"More sense than you."

"A man walks in here, and what does he see? Imagine someone comin' in right now. He opens the door, he sees Tessa dancin' back here on the stage, those tits movin' the way they move, and he sees the bar back here too. This is where the drinks are at, way over here. And what does he do? He stops at the first seat in the house. That can only be one of two things, Daisy. Pure insanity or pure calculation, because of the ATM."

"Or he's just nervous, so he sat down right away."

"Nervous guys don't come in here alone at 2:26 on a Monday, Daisy-girl."

"You don't know everyone," she said. "Don't act like you do."

"If they're walkin' into a strip club, I know 'em," he said. "Oh, I know 'em."

"Says the guy who claims he doesn't like strip clubs."

"Well if you'd let me finish," said Kenny.

"That sounds familiar, doesn't it?"

"You're clever today."

"Usually am."

83

"You are. You really are." Kenny sipped his whiskey, his stare drifting from the brim of his glass to Tessa whirling on the pole. Something was different about her routine today, but he couldn't quite nail it down.

"She get a haircut or something?"

"Usually wears heels," said Daisy.

"There it is," said Kenny.

"Twisted her ankle. She's been doing Capoeira."

"The fuck's Capoeira?"

"Some kind of Brazilian dancing that's like karate too. It's a form of dance, but there's a self-defense element to it. I don't know, really. It's like graceful fighting or something."

Kenny shifted Daisy from his left thigh to his right. "Darren still havin' his way with her?"

Daisy nodded.

"That guy's a walkin' fuckin' mistake, you know that? I mean, look at her. Barefoot."

"She hurt it doing Capoeira," said Daisy.

"Yea, but she's only doin' karate ballet because he's smackin' her around. Come on, big picture."

Leonard entered. They couldn't see him yet, but they heard his cane tapping the floor. It wasn't until he walked by the ATM, its faint yellow light prying him out of the black, that he became real to them. He breathed heavily, his forehead glistening with sweat.

"Leonard," said Kenny.

"There's my Lenny," said Daisy.

"It's hotter than a Hindu's jockstrap out there," said Leonard. He plopped down beside them and whistled to Fawn for a rum and Coke. "Don't be shy with the ice."

The song came to an end, and Tessa walked off stage. Kenny kept a close eye on her bare feet. He could hear them sticking to the tile floor as she paced into the dressing room. No fuckin' shoes, he thought. It wouldn't do. He decided that he'd have to have a word with Darren.

"Well?" asked Daisy.

"Well what?" responded Kenny.

"You hate it here…"

"Oh, shit, yea. I do. I fuckin' hate strip clubs in general, really. Now that I've been thinkin'."

"Me too," said Leonard.

"No, I'm serious. We've been discussin' this, Lenny," said Kenny.

"Trying to, at least," said Daisy.

"Yea, I've been gettin' around to it," Kenny said. "It's something I've been thinkin' about though, in a wider sense. I hate strip clubs, I really do. I mean, look around. Who in their right mind would wanna come in here?"

"On a day like today," said Leonard. "No choice."

"Sure, the AC's nice," Kenny continued, "but it's a fuckin' dungeon in here. The kind of place you'd put a terrorist in if you wanted to break him. If you wanted him to lose his sense of reality and give in and tell ya which cave all of his jihadi pals were campin' out in."

"And yet you're here," said Daisy.

"Let me finish," said Kenny.

"You don't look so good, Lenny," said Fawn as she set down his rum and Coke.

"The heat," said Lenny. "It's something."

"Well I loaded you up with ice, honey. A whole lot of ice."

"Fawn, we're tryin' to discuss something here," said Kenny.

"Rude," said Daisy, slapping Kenny's thigh.

"I don't like strip clubs," Kenny continued. "I hate the dark, I hate the way your girls' legs make that sound when you're doin' your thing up there—when it gets caught, the friction, you know, on the pole—and I hate that there's a way all strip clubs tend to be. How they make you feel a little shitty when you're in them. It's like everything in here is sendin' you a message, tellin' you this isn't such a good thing we're doin', that we oughtta be somewhere else, where the lights are on. I could go for a different feel, I guess is what I'm saying. Why not have some lights, some nice shit on the walls—"

"There's paintings," said Daisy.

"Yea, and we can't fuckin' see 'em," said Kenny.

"The ones in the bathroom, you can see those," said Leonard.

"Dressing room too," added Fawn.

"Yea, 'cause there's lights. And maybe that's a piece of what I'm gettin' at. The bathrooms aren't supposed to be the nicest places in the fuckin' building," said Kenny. "There's something backward in that."

"There's something backward about you of all people, Kenny, talking down about this place," said Daisy.

"I'm not talkin' down," he said. "I'm just talkin'. And thinkin'. And what I think is that I don't like it all that much in here. But what I do like is strippers. Hate strip clubs, like strippers."

"You love strippers," said Fawn as she headed back to the bar.

"I do," he admitted, squeezing Daisy's left hip. "But I guess what I really mean is, I wish you girls picked somewhere else to hang out. If all the strippers got together in some other place—like, anywhere. Let's say a Chinese restaurant for instance, like over at Chen's— then, Christ, I'd be on some kind of 24/7 wonton diet. Might even look into maybe learnin' Mandarin."

"I'm sure that would go over fantastically," said Daisy. "Us marching into Chen's, taking our tops off, getting up on the tables. They'd love that, Kenny, yea. Great idea."

"First of all, you'd be surprised. As long as there's no kids in there, they just might let it go on for a while, those cooks, just to see some skin. Most people like that kind of mayhem, they just don't admit it. But then there'd be that one person who had their kids there or some Straight Sally who'd call the cops. They'd come eventually, yea, but you'd have some time to do your thing, trust me. Those cooks in there, they'd let it play out. They wouldn't tell a soul."

"Fried rice and dancing girls," said Leonard. "I'm there."

"Me too," said Kenny. "But that's not what I meant anyhow. What I meant is, it's not about the strippin' either way. It has nothin' to do with it. The takin'-your-clothes-off is irrelevant. It's about the *types of girls* that strippers tend to be. That's what I like. That's my main theme here. Even if the girls kept their clothes on, stayed fully covered up head to toe, I'd go wherever those girls are. I'd be there, rain or shine. Because it's about them as people. That's the beauty of it."

"You're so full of shit, Kenny. You know that?" said Daisy.

"Hey now," said Leonard.

"No, if you're not gunna say it, I will," continued Daisy. "You're the horniest man in the building, all day every day. To have you sit here and act like you're not in here for the ass and the tits is just a load of bullshit. It's so untrue that it's retarded, honestly. It's not even worth trying to say."

"A few zingers there, Daisy," said Leonard. "Couple keepers."

"And you act like all strippers are the same kinds of people," she said.

"You are," said Kenny.

"Yea, in one main way—we strip. We take our fucking clothes off, Kenny."

"But there are certain qualities that make certain people more willing to do it," said Kenny.

"Winners," said Leonard.

"You would never give anyone in here, including myself, the time of day if we always had our clothes on," said Daisy. "I mean, shit, I wouldn't even know you,

Kenny. We would have never met. But guess what? We did. And you might not be into the decor or the pitch-black, but that just proves my point even more. That's how much you love it. You're willing to be in here for twelve hours a day in a place you insist is miserable if it means you get to stare at us in these fucking outfits and have me sit this ass on your lap."

"What'd I tell ya? Winners," said Leonard.

Kenny smiled and drank his whiskey and nodded, his grin getting wider and wider until he could put words to it: "That's the good shit, Daisy. That's what I'm talkin' about. I love hearin' shit like that. The goddamn truth, the gospel. Those smacks in the face, knockin' me down a peg, lettin' me know who the fuck I really am. That, my darling, is why I'm here. There's just no tellin' what the fuck you ladies are gunna say. No tellin' whatsoever. But you're also wrong too. Slightly off, at least. Because I'm guaranteein' you, it doesn't matter whether those tits are out and shakin' or if they're tucked away, I'll be here to listen to you talk that sweetness. I'll be sittin' right here. Me and Leonard."

"Better if they're out," said Leonard. "If we're casting votes."

"At least you're honest about it," said Daisy, rubbing Leonard's bald head. She found her feet and finished off her martini. "I think I'm up."

"There she is," said Kenny.

"Yee-haw," said Leonard.

"Maybe I'll keep my top on," she said. "After Kenny's big revelation and all."

89

"Not an option," said Kenny.

"Yea, don't be like that," said Leonard.

Daisy made her way up onto the stage. The music started, and off came her top.

"You two seem good," said Leonard.

"Surviving," said Kenny.

"Divorce off the table?"

"Never fully."

Kenny heard feet gripping the floor before Tess even exited the dressing room.

"Tess," he said, waving her over.

"What's up?" asked Tess.

"The feet," he said.

"I know. It's just for tonight," she said. "I rolled my ankle. In a dance class."

"Capoeira," said Kenny.

She nodded.

"How about some socks? Just while you're walking around," said Kenny.

"Well actually," said Leonard. "Before you go covering those things up, how about a dance for old Lenny-boy?" He gave Kenny a look, requesting permission. "It's hotter than hell out today."

Kenny nodded. The socks could wait a song or two.

My Last Drink

"My first beer is my last," I said as we made a left onto Bonito.

But I knew he wouldn't understand exactly what I meant. It would take time to explain it to him. Ten or fifteen minutes, maybe. He'd probably appreciate some distraction from the monotony of driving anyway. Plus, I could sense that he was intelligent, the type of man who would not only comprehend what I meant but also appreciate it. He might even like me once I fleshed it all out for him. He would get it. So I took him twelve hours back in time, when I had my last drink.

I have about thirty beers each night. Sometimes I have fewer, around twenty-eight or twenty-nine. But I never have more. There are my eighteen beers from the Citgo station, and Gary knows to only serve me twelve, so that's my limit. Eighteen at home, twelve at the Watermark. Yes, I could save money and just buy a thirty rack, but it's a twenty-minute walk from the gas station and my arms can't handle the weight. Plus, I'm supposed to like the socialization at the bar, so sometimes I do. Anyway, I knew I had to make that

91

clear to my driver. Thirty beers per night, that's what I drink.

He nodded at me in the rearview mirror. One of those fatherly nods, somewhere between disappointment and approval, a mystery. But I think he liked it. My commitment, that is. The way I am. It's not that easy to drink thirty beers. And to make a routine of it, to center my day around it—no one in their right mind can just brush that aside. But he did his best to.

"And then what?" he asked.

I apologized for getting so into the beers, my tendencies. I explained to him that I knew he would be impressed by it, by my commitment. He did one of those nods again, a carbon copy of the last one. I realized that these might be his thing, these nods. I couldn't help but think how interesting it was. A nod, a most straightforward gesture with a definite meaning—yes. But yes was only a fraction of the meaning of this man's nod. A small fraction. Why couldn't he just say something one way or the other, or admit that my drinking was remarkable? Everyone usually does. But the thirty beers weren't even the real story here. I just wanted to give him some color and let him know this wasn't an accident. I've worked for this.

"Those first twelve beers, I drink at my kitchen table."

"That leaves six," he said, making a right onto Fourth.

"Yea, those are for after the Watermark."

He just kept driving. Not an ounce of respect.

"Thirty-two minutes," I said. "I drink those opening twelve in about thirty-two minutes."

He did one of those nods again. It really was his thing.

"Actually, not *about* thirty-two minutes. Thirty-two minutes on the dot. Exactly thirty-two minutes, every day."

Silence. This guy's one of those prideful types who only give compliments to their kids, and only because they have to, because society says he probably should. If he doesn't have children, I'd be willing to bet he's never given any credit to anyone for anything. He's probably never had twelve beers in thirty-two minutes, let alone done it consistently with a serious purpose. These are the worst types of people. Subtle folks. I'd rather he just come out and say that he thinks he's better than me and everyone else. It's better to be outright terrible than possibly bad. Just tell me who I'm looking at.

"That's a lot of beer," he said, eyeing me in the rearview mirror. His eyebrows went skyward, but not long enough to definitively tell me anything. It was like a man who wanted you to think, only for a moment, that what you do might matter to him. Must have taken him decades to develop this level of condescension.

I hit him back with one of his nods, even emulating his eyebrow movement. I thought I matched him perfectly, but he thought nothing of it. I guess it's hard to distinguish between nods, but to me they matter; our little nuances and idiosyncrasies, they're the only line between me and the world—the flavor. Otherwise people can say we're all in this thing together.

He was silent for a while, and I sensed that it was almost time to tell my story, the real bulk of it, anyway. The longer a silence persists, the more powerful the words need to be to shatter it. Anything won't do. And I was sitting on verbal dynamite, so I let the quiet build. Anyone who's afraid of lasting silence is really just scared that they don't have the firepower to shatter it. Not an issue here.

"I drink those twelve beers from eleven in the morning until eleven thirty-two. My clock is slightly behind though, so it's almost always eleven twenty-nine when I toss my twelfth empty into the trash. I don't crush the cans, either. Otherwise their size is inconsistent. If you don't crush them, it takes about forty-five of them to fill the trash can. If they're crushed, there's no telling how many it's gunna take before having to take out the trash. Easier to keep track that way. It's amazing, really, how much room cans take up when you don't stack them neatly. But I guess you could look at it the other way around too. It's beautiful how many cans fit into a case when they're carefully stacked."

"Then you went to the bar," he said.

"I *go* to the bar. I went today, yes, but I always go."

So strange. Why was he nudging me on? I wanted to tell him that I can handle more than thirty beers if I had to. But if I did more, there would be nothing else. No sleeping, no eating, no talking. And it would be nearly impossible not to talk. I might choose talking over beers. That would be a diabolical thought experiment. I love to talk.

"I get to the bar at eleven forty, after those twelve in my kitchen, and Gary has one waiting for me. The bartender."

"Gary Henderson," he said.

I'm not sure if it was a question, but I nodded one of my nods. A straightforward yes. Then I got to the heart of the matter. I explained to him that at the Watermark I drink twelve beers and stay until four thirty. Give or take, that's about two-and-a-half beers per hour, a casual pace.

Of course, I could drink more. To take it slow like this, it's pure discipline. It's like a game of basketball against your twelve-year-old nephew. You don't crush him, but you win. And Gary, he helps me take it easy too.

That's the wonderful thing about bars: you get to talk. There's always a bartender. You may not like him, but he's there. And he may not like listening, but he can't leave. People love to complain about how much drinkers drink and talk, but talking is one of the only ways to drink less. Take your pick. That's irrelevant with Gary though. I like him, and he likes me.

I once went to a bar in JFK airport. One of these worthless modern establishments. Very clean, everything as it should be. And there was no bartender. Just an iPad to choose my drink. Then a server would deliver a beer and disappear. When I tried to talk to her, she kept it brief. Her not wanting to listen wasn't the issue. It was that she could leave. So I drank thirty-one beers and played solitaire on the iPad.

I explained to the man driving that on this particular day—today—nothing was particular. Gary had a cold one waiting when I got to the Watermark, we talked, and I had my twelve. I told him how I love it when Gary cuts up the limes because he never talks and interrupts me while he does it. Lime time was my time.

"That's how you cut a finger off," I said.

Another nod.

I felt like I was being unnecessarily redundant, like I was repeating myself. So I thought about it. No, no, I wasn't. I knew I wasn't. It was just that I needed to arrive at the crux of what I meant by all of this, what the whole deal was.

"The reason I drink the way I do is because that's how I've always done it. Twelve in my kitchen, twelve at the bar, then six back in my kitchen. If it was any other way, I would be fooling myself."

"Routine," he said, as if he understood what I meant. But he didn't. It's so easy to hide behind concision. Some mistake brevity of speech for wisdom, but that's not at all true. He says one word and thinks it conveys a thousand. But there's only one way to get a thought out, and that's to say it. Actions only speak louder than words if you can't find the right words. And I wasn't going to let him go on acting like he grasped what I meant.

"If you live your life the same way, day after day, you are a singular action. You are it."

He nodded and stared at me in the mirror. It was a taunting gaze, like he was holding back a smirk, the kind of expression a dumb person gives a smart person when they're trying to shame profundity. It's like he could not admit that what I said was beyond his reach but undeniably compelling.

"If every day I drink thirty beers, what is the difference between beer number one and beer number thirty?"

Another silence. He was growing apathetic because he couldn't understand, like someone who tosses away a Van Gogh from the attic because they don't know it's worth millions. He took a left onto Redondo. It would have probably been best to let it fade, to accept the fact that this man lacked the intellectual capacity to comprehend me. Even if he could conceptualize what I meant, he wouldn't appreciate it. Understanding is far easier than appreciating.

"My first drink is my last drink. Don't you see that? Time itself is a human illusion. Everything is really unfolding at once. This very moment, your birth, your death, your wedding night, the 1988 World Series— they're all right now. The only real way to embrace that is to live repetitively. To not dupe yourself into thinking today isn't tomorrow and tomorrow isn't yesterday. People like to think that winter is its own thing, like it's not summer. But if everything is really unfolding at once, there's no differentiation. Is that too much for you to grasp?"

Silence.

A long one.

My driver took a sledgehammer to it.

"As I've said, yes, I get it, Billy. Time is relative. I know the story."

Something clicked. I realized that he knew exactly what I meant. My first drink is my last, and my last is my first. And there was wisdom in his nods. They were not a mystery but rather the most concise response, the quickest way to let me get back to talking. And I love to talk. He knew this. I think he knew all of it.

We pulled into the Citgo station. The Powerball was up to $103 million. Yesterday it was at $81 million, the day before $58 million. But someone will win, and it will start all over again.

"You pissed on Clara's front door again," said my driver as he pulled into a parking spot.

"I do that."

It wasn't a question, but he nodded. I felt as though I'd wasted my time with him, like I spent every second saying things I've said before. But then it dawned on me that this was quite fitting, actually, to have repeated myself. If I were to have said new things or concocted some cute story, I'd only be fooling myself into thinking that now isn't later, and that I might have a different day tomorrow.

Summerhaze got out of the driver's seat and swung open my door. "I'd say don't do it again, but—"

"I won't. I promise," I said, exiting the car.

"Sure you do," he said.

"I mean it."

"I know you do, Billy. Doesn't mean you'll remember it though."

Officer Summerhaze unlocked my handcuffs as I peered in the Citgo station windows. Omar was behind the counter, the beer fridge glowing along the back wall. Wonderful lights. Everyone talks so fondly of lights, but they're really only good when they show us what we want to see.

"Goodnight, Billy," said Summerhaze.

He gave a subtle wave as he got back into his cruiser. I didn't wave back, but he knew it wasn't out of animosity. I never wave.

I'll see him soon.

I grabbed my eighteen pack and set it on the counter. Omar didn't say a word. He knows me well.

I Am Not

I beat cancer three years ago. But the day I learned I had cancer was far more emotional than the day I was confirmed cancerfree. To be living and find out that you're dying is to have your sense of time destroyed. All of your plans, all of those sunny days you imagined on the other side of your hard work—they vanish with a fews words spoken under fluorescent light. Now, that's not to say that I believe life generally gets better. But to be human is to hope it will.

When you boil it down, it's really not so important that your life improves. But it's essential for you to be free to imagine so. This is key in any arrangement, be it life, your career, your marriage, or your irritable bowel syndrome. So long as you can convince yourself there are greener pastures, you can keep trekking through the dirt. This freedom—the right to delusion— is the defining factor of human life.

Statistically, the percentage of fulfilled human dreams is negligible when compared to the overall number of dreams we cook up. After all, most dreams die with the dreamer, and he or she never even became aware of the fact that these aspirations were merely the gasoline on a journey with no end point. We run on hope. And this hoping, this holding of unrealistic visions of the future, is more important than the blood in our veins.

I think of my cancer diagnosis like the universe playing an accordion. Death decided on a different note, condensing the trajectory of my life from a hundred years into forty. It recently dawned on me that even my long-held assumption that I'd be alive in ten years, let alone sixty, was a form of wishful thinking. Normally we like to think of hope as being a longing for something better. But even the basic expectation that your life will maintain the status quo, that you will be permitted to keep breathing, is a form of naive hope. The universe doesn't owe us anything, yet we seem to expect the world of it. We want the gift of a long and disease-free life, with anything less being deemed bad luck. But that's a lazy conclusion when dissected. To be alive at all, by any measure of fortune, is astronomically good luck. It's a blessing beyond calculation.

Even a short life is a miracle when weighed against all possible outcomes. To die young, therefore, is not so much bad luck as it is the dissolution of our childish hope that we deserve to live into old age and quietly pass away in a king-size bed. That vision you created in your mind of your eighty-two-year-old self smiling and drinking coffee and passing on indispensable wisdom to your grandkids is as delusional as the plan me and my girlfriend had to start a pottery studio. Both were useful ideas while they kept you moving, but that's all they were—ideas; your own flavor of hope. Now, if you live long enough, it'll be life that crushes that hope. But an early death sentence will do it far more swiftly; no letting you down easy. One genetic mutation will strip your goals naked and expose them for the pipe dreams they always were. Your dearest dreams were laughable impossibilities.

I remember the day after the bad news, I was staring into the mirror and beginning to realize that my body was not my companion. We were not in this together. I'd always leaned on a sense of symbiosis, a trust that my heart and my lungs and my pancreas knew what my brain wanted and would help me get it. But I had been betrayed by my own biology despite doing everything in my power to optimize my own health.

There I was, thirty-three years old, spending so much of my cash and enthusiasm on organic food and supplements only to end up as one of those people who nature decides to kill off as a reminder that death can show up at the front door quicker than fish oil pills from Amazon. I can eat my non-GMO vegetables. I can run my three miles a day. I can hope for the best. But I am living proof that diseases don't check your résumé.

I was walking up the same stairs I'd walked up two years earlier with the same eerie feeling. It was back. I could feel it. I could hear it. Hospitals all have the same subtle echo about them that makes every action, every shuffle of feet or ding of an elevator, more dramatic. All things auditory have their life spans doubled in this fluorescent prison. A half-off sale on terror. It's not enough to just get through something; it gets played back.

"You look like you need some help," said a nurse.

I didn't. I knew exactly where I was going. I had just stopped at the top of the stairs to gather myself and was thinking that if I had Benny's ears I could probably hear the echo of my heartbeat bouncing off the white tiles and endless hallways and MRI machines, finding every nook and surface, only to race back and smack me in the soul.

"That's correct. I need you guys to save me," I said with a chuckle.

"We're usually pretty good at that," she responded, smiling.

"That's what I hear. I know where I'm going though. Thank you."

"Have a good day," she said.

"You too."

Usually.

She could have said—"We *are* pretty good at that"— but she didn't. *Usually* pretty good, that's what she said. Healthcare providers have a practicality about them that would serve most of us well. Because they know the truth—not everyone gets out of here alive. There is a final echo.

Sometimes I think people in the medical field, especially doctors and nurses who work with the terminally ill, live for the fact that they're the purveyors of death. They chose their careers not so much to fight death but to be the closest among us to

103

it, the sole messengers on behalf of the end. Doctors don't drudge through four years of med school and three years of residency to become more open-minded; they do it to learn concrete answers. And they want to be the ones to deliver them. Only the white coats can be the heralds of death. Take a seat.

The waiting room was brighter than I remembered. At first, I thought they might have added some lights, but I realized that it was the floor. There used to be dark-blue tiles scattered among the white ones, but they've been removed. All white tiles and I couldn't help but think there was some intention behind such a design change. Hospitals don't typically hide their agendas very well. Hallways say *Do not stop, just pass on through*—they're always white and bleak and uninviting, with the doors ajar just enough to remind you that this is no place for loitering. This is a hotel for the damned. Waiting rooms, on the other hand, are where they throw a dash of color, some fake plants, a few stock images in cheap plastic frames. And they only do this because of their own inefficiency; people have to wait. If hospitals could treat every patient and have them out the door before the next one was waiting, they would. They'd waste no space on areas that seem tailored to say *This is where you sit, but don't get comfortable.*

As for the all-white tile in the waiting room, I feel like they're trying to tell us something. It's a kind of hallway-waiting room hybrid, a place where no one would want to sit unless they had to. Might as well have a sign on the wall: *Let's just get this over with.* It's like they're trying to discourage patients from bringing friends and family, which makes sense. Unless you're a paying guest, hospitals don't want you there. Visitors don't pay an entry fee. Only the dying keep the fluorescent lights on.

When I looked around the room, I saw two types of patients. Some were smiling, laughing among family, and I had to assume it was their first time. They hadn't gotten the memo yet that this was not a place for congregation. There was a large family off in the corner who fell into this category. Superb acting. They should have been on a stage. The whole family tree—Mom, Dad, Grandpa, kids, grandkids—was trying to make light of the situation, drinking coffee and telling stories, as if horrific news wasn't awaiting them beyond the wooden door.

Then there were the depressed, the hopeless. Or hopeful, I should say. There was a woman near the reception desk, her eyes empty, who could have been the poster child for this population. She picked up three different magazines only to set them down moments later. She would get one paragraph into an article before asking herself the almighty question—What's the point? This question starts with small things, everyday tasks. But once a person knows they're dying, it bleeds into every facet of their life. Nothing seems worth pursuing. These are the same folks who think they've run into bad luck; still clinging to the delusion that there is a definite set of years on Earth that a human being is entitled to. A delusion in the form of hope.

On one side of the coin we have the placebo group, the happy half who thinks swallowing the optimism pill and feeding riddles to the grandkids can keep their plans intact. If they just stay busy and smile, the thought of the grave can't sneak in. That trip to Thailand they had on the books, it's still happening. So is the wedding next August. If they just imagine a positive outcome, they increase the chances of one manifesting itself. That's the idea, at least.

And then there's the other half, the nocebo group. These are the ones who, if we're to believe the power of thought, are expediting their own death, their negative thoughts pressing the fast-forward button on their existence. They're crushed by their impending expiration, with all of their goals and dreams and tomorrows dissolving in their minds. The present is no longer seeming like the center point between the past and the future. Their memories seem vast when compared to the short and hazy life they're struggling to see ahead. Goddamnit, they've been shorted, swindled by the universe. And they still haven't figured out that their baseline of what a life ought to be is completely arbitrary. They're yet to arrive at the truth that life has no definition, and death no standards. Someone must pay for this. They may blame God. They may blame nature. But there will be no trial.

I seemed to be the only one in the waiting room who fell directly in the middle of these two crowds. I was dying, yet I wasn't trying to evade this thought. Nor did

I feel cheated. During my first bout with cancer I fell in love with a quote by Epicurus, which was put on his gravestone: *Non fui, fui, non sum, non curo.* He was straightforward about his own demise: *I was not, I was, I am not, I do not care.* Some lives are short, some are long, but most never happen. It is a wild blessing to even have the chance to despair.

I've sat many times among the dying. I've swallowed placebos and nocebos and every pill in between. I've scorned death, nestled up to it, bowed down to it. I've been through the darkness, heard the echoes, and eventually walked out that wooden door cancer-free. And while I wouldn't recommend fighting cancer to anyone, if you're forced to, should you beat it, the knowledge gained is worth its weight in gold.

The wooden door swung open and Patricia emerged. She didn't have to call out my name. She simply waved. It was back.

"How's Meghan? Did you two find a storefront yet?" asked Patricia.

"She's good," I said. "Same old, really. We're still looking for a spot though."

"Fingers crossed."

I nodded and crossed my fingers.

"Patience is key," she said.

"Indeed it is," I said.

She opened her mouth to say something, but anxiety stole her words. It was like she wanted to tell me the bad news right then and there but knew it wasn't her place. After all, nurses are the soldiers. They do all the leg work. Ask the questions. Draw the blood. Run the tests. They know the truth before the doctor swoops in to steal the glory.

"Dr. Henning will be right with you."

I noticed a small golden crucifix necklace as she pivoted and headed for the door. It shut, then echoed. That crucifix was new. I never saw it in any of my times coming here. I couldn't for the life of me imagine having a religious awakening while working in here—a death chapel—so I assumed she must have been a lifelong believer. I have to confess that when I was first diagnosed, I tried to believe in God. Or gods. There can be great value in accepting an absurdity, even subconsciously knowing so, if it brings wisdom.

Now, mine was not necessarily the God of Catholicism or Islam or any of the established religions, but just a deity or gang of deities in general. I realized, however, that it was never about Him or Her or it or them. It was about me. During this period, I was still in my hopeful phase, wanting more of this thing we call life, adamant that I'd been hosed. While most people won't admit it, this is obviously the primary motivation for religiosity. Folks don't want to love their neighbor or avoid bearing false witness; they want to keep breathing. Hell is merely a sneaky way to make things look less self-centered. People can say "I don't want that" about the hell instead of insisting "I really want that" about the heaven. But this is like people insisting they bought a luxury vehicle for the safety features—to avoid accidents—as opposed to admitting they wanted to be envied. Give people a chance to appear humble and meek, and they'll empty the bank and die for it.

I heard Dr. Henning's footsteps in the hall. Each had an auditory disciple.

This was one of those moments when death brings perspective. I sensed that the accordion was about to be compressed, that there was about to be a genocide of tomorrows. Sometimes it's as though the mind knows it's about to lose years so it churns out as many ideas as it can and lets you decide which ones to embrace in your waning days. I did not deserve a god. I was not on someone's agenda. This was it.

My last ounce of hope slipped away. To hope is to be human, I told myself; so to lose all hope is the most ready one can be for the casket. I was ahead of the curve.

Dr. Henning swung open the door: "Hello, David."

"How are ya, Doc?" I said.

"I'm doing just fine, David. Patricia tells me that you're not?"

I shook my head. He knew what this meant.

"What exactly is going on?" he asked.

"Same issues. I think it's back."

He typed away on his computer. The amount of gadgets in these examination rooms was unfathomable. A hundred devices humming away. Black noise. They've invented so many ways to tell you that you're a goner.

Dr. Henning took a seat beside me. This is what they do when there's bad news. A doctor doesn't sit down, take a deep breath, and make a ceremony of telling someone they're in perfectly good health. A herald of death—he lived for this.

"David, I know we've been through this before, but…" He removed his glasses and touched my shoulder. "There's nothing wrong with you. When you say the cancer is back, it worries me, David. It really does. It's not a good sign. I don't know how to tell you this any more bluntly—you've never had cancer. No tests or scans have ever shown any sign of it. Just about every symptom you've ever come in here with has been purely psychological. And don't take that as something bad. It's a good thing. You're healthy, David. Young and healthy, with a lot of life left in you. But I think it would really help you, like I've suggested, to see a psychiatrist. I can connect you with one if you'd like. It's what I think you should do."

"Can you just run some tests?" I said.

"David, I'm sure you're fine," he insisted. The arrogance. God forbid I knew more than he did.

"Can you just do your job, please?" I said.

"David, again, I can run some blood tests, but I'm going to almost guarantee you that nothing will turn up. And as you know, I'm a general practitioner, so this is as far as it will go. Unless you have some actual symptom that we can pinpoint, I can't just go referring you to an oncologist. It doesn't work like that."

"I know how it works," I said.

"Okay, David. If it'll put you at ease, we'll take some blood."

He again touched my shoulder and headed for the door. He said he was *sure that I'm fine*. A euphoria crept over me that was better than any of the drugs they could pump me full of in this place. Cancer could not touch me. The accordion stretched, tomorrows materialized, the countless echoes of Dr. Henning's departure became a welcomed choir singing the good news: I was a lucky one.

"Don't let him lick that," said my girlfriend.

"Why not?" I asked.

"It has cacao in it. Probably enough to kill him."

"Sorry, Benny. What's good for us ain't good for pups, buddy." I tossed my empty smoothie into a trash can. We were on our way to Fourth Street, where all the trendy shops are, to check out a potential storefront for our pottery studio. Opening the studio has been a plan of ours for years. To be transparent, that plan has been a consistent one for her, but an on-again, off-again one for myself. I was planning to die within six months—signing a two-year lease wasn't in the game plan. That was more tomorrows than I could afford to think about. I never told my girlfriend about my condition though, because I knew she'd consider it what the doctors considered it—an illness. But to be dying has tremendous upside, especially when you're not.

There were about sixty people walking the sidewalks, and if I had to guess, none of them thought they were dying. A real shame, a waste of talent. They were mostly young and middle-aged and filled with hope. They haven't felt the accordion squeeze. They think there's some way that life ought to go. Lucky

111

ones. If each of them was, as an experiment, duped and convinced they'd be dead in six months, they would all come out the other side with a wisdom that most folks don't acquire until they're old and gray. They would feel unlucky, then apathetic, then delighted to feel at all. Most people only get one chance to die, with the perspective they gain from it going with them into the dirt. It's only those of us who can figure out a way to die over and over who can unlock life's secrets. The white coats call it hypochondria. I call it reincarnation.

"Exposed brick," said my girlfriend.

"She loves exposed brick," I said to the Realtor.

"Well there's no shortage of bricks in here," he said.

The place was beautiful. Reality outdid our dreams. My girlfriend and I didn't have to say a word. We both knew—this was the place. The best architecture is that which feels like it has a storied past but also has stories to come; a building that has long been loved and has a lot more to give. The years played out in my head.

"Well? What do we think?"

"It's perfect," said my girlfriend.

"It really is," I said.

My phone rang, and I excused myself out.

"Hello?" I said.

"Hello, David, this is Meredith. From Dr. Henning's office."

"Hi, Meredith."

"I'm just calling about your tests, the blood tests. Are you busy?"

"I am not," I said.

I heard her clicking and typing and doing things in the fluorescent light. The echoes always sounded different over the phone. My girlfriend smiled at me from inside. With every second, a brick disappeared off the walls. Years melted away. The accordion was about to play a new note—I will probably live into old age; or die tomorrow. One of his heralds, she took a breath. I was doomed.

A Long Line of Mainly Heathen

I was the last person in line for only a few seconds until footsteps arrived behind me. It was a woman. She had to be in her eighties, perhaps even nineties. The hunch in her back blended with the desert ridges behind her— she was a living, breathing land form; the horizon brought to life. And she was smiling.

"I'm Ruth," said the woman.

"Richard," I said.

She settled in line behind me and admired a nearby cactus.

"Any idea how far up this goes?" I asked.

She leaned to her right, peering up the line: "As far as I can see."

A young Asian man jogged up and became the last in line. Drenched in sweat, he started clamoring away in his native language, his ramblings becoming more and more distraught, echoing off the rocky hills to our left.

I thought about yelling back.

"Ruth." She pointed to herself, then repeated: "Ruth."

Then she gently touched my chest: "Richard."

114

"Richard," I said with a nod.

The man took some time to catch his breath. "Li," he said.

"Nǐ hǎo, Li," said Ruth. The two had a short conversation, none of which I understood, then Ruth returned her focus to me: "One of my best friends was from Beijing."

I gazed toward the front of the line. There had to be at least a few hundred thousand people ahead of us, maybe more. That the line even had a beginning in the traditional sense was purely hypothetical. If it did, it was too far away to see, beyond the horizon. But Ruth went on smiling and thinking nothing of anything. She was content in the face of mystery. I did my best to match her state of calm and contain my panic.

"What's happening here?" I asked.

"Pardon?"

"This line. Do you know what the deal is?"

"Oh, I'm afraid not, dear," she said. "It seems to me like one big heap of people, some of whom are standing relatively still and some of whom are moving. Me and you, Richard, I believe we just made the transition from the moving line to the standing line. And I don't know about you, but I like this line much better."

I stepped away and surveyed the back of the line. It wasn't until then that I realized what she meant by the moving line. There were already hundreds of people standing behind us, but beyond them was an endless string of human beings walking toward us.

I tapped the shoulder of the man ahead of me, a Japanese gentleman who had to be over one hundred.

"Konnichiwa," he said.

"Do you speak English by any chance?"

"Yes, my friend. The name's Yusuke. How can I help you?" His delivery was slow and methodical. He adjusted his bow tie and yanked up his suspenders as if ready to play tour guide.

"Do you know what's going on?"

"I can help with anything but that," he said to me with a chuckle as Ruth leaned in.

"I'm Ruth." She didn't shake his hand, but the two held a gaze for a moment.

"Well, hi there, Ruthie," said Yusuke. "Aren't you a diamond in the rough."

"It's not so rough here," she said.

"Agreed. Perhaps it was the wrong phrase for the occasion."

"It was half right," said Ruth.

"When did you get here? Into the line," I interrupted.

"A minute or two before you," said Yusuke.

I gestured toward the back. "And you two, did you see the people in front of you and behind you?"

"Oh, yes," said Ruth. "I was just behind you, Richard. At times close enough to reach out and touch you. I was going to say hello, but you were in such a rush to get here to the standing line that I thought it'd be a shame to slow you down. I thought maybe you knew where you were headed."

"I was headed here. To this line," I said.

"The standing line," said Ruth.

"Yes, the standing line," I snapped. "But I had no idea what it was. I just...I saw it."

"Who were you yelling at the whole time?" she asked.

"It wasn't *at* anyone," I said.

"The echoes sounded nice," said Ruth.

"Always do," said Yusuke.

"I was just frustrated, that's all."

"Can't blame you, Richard," said Yusuke. "But if I may say so myself, there's no sense in cracking the whip if there's no guilty party. Sure, that cracking noise is nice and crisp, but after a while you realize you're just wasting energy."

"It must have been on purpose," I said.

"Pardon?" asked Ruth.

"The fact that I couldn't see anyone walking—there must be a reason. I mean, I didn't see anyone ahead of me or behind me or anything. There was no moving line in front of me. I was alone with just the desert. Then, out of nowhere...this line. The standing line."

"Hopefully we can get some answers if we just hang tight," said Ruth.

"That's the spirit, Ruthie," said Yusuke. "And if it's any comfort to you, Richie, you didn't miss out on much. The view only changes for the lead dog, as they say. And my behind isn't much to look at."

After a few months, we realized a few things about the line. First of all, hunger and thirst did not exist. We needed no sustenance. Nor did fatigue exist, which I believed had to do with our sleeping routine. Once the sun set, everyone went to sleep. This wasn't an organized rule or anything—it just happened naturally. And one might think the desert ground would be uncomfortable, but the rest had been the best I'd ever experienced, with no nightmares or tossing and turning. The same went for the entire line. The sleep was so perfect that Yusuke insisted we call it something else, something like *absence*.

We settled into a rhythm. It astonished me how much time opened up when meals were unnecessary and we were never tired. The not-eating part added an extra hour or two of free time to everyone's day. But the lack of fatigue made me realize how much time in my life I'd spent longing for my next slumber because my previous one didn't get the job done. The line eliminated the perpetual and unwinnable game of catching up on sleep that is inherent in a human life.

So time was easy to come by. Based on normal standards, there's far too much of it. And as for what we could do with it, there was only one option—we waited. But some refused. Many times a day, someone walked or sprinted toward the front of the line, cutting the rest of us. This happened much more in the first couple of days, when people weren't used to all the waiting and eventual known risks.

Because—without fail—these people disappeared. Line-cutters simply vanished each night once everyone went to sleep. Upon waking, there was no sign of them.

Some people still cut despite knowing it meant their own demise, and for them I present three theories.

One—insanity: The line had gotten to them. Two—purpose: They ran with the blind hope that they were close enough to our destination to see it before the sun went down. Or three—suicide: The most common. They assumed vanishing was the final end, and they preferred that to the line itself. This made little sense. Enough people in the line took that same approach in their normal lives and ended up here.

When you kill yourself, regardless of what anyone tells you, there's no guarantee that you're really killing yourself. We only call death *death* because it's the furthest we can see. And should there be something beyond it, which obviously there is, it's for everyone. There is no doorman. There are no prerequisites for this; no dress code, no entrance exam. All you have to do is die.

"Good morning, Richard," said Yusuke.

"Morning, Yusuke."

The sunrise was beautiful, its rays refracting through the dew on the chaparral yuccas and creosote bushes. A cluster of silhouettes blew across the sand in the distance.

"Coyotes," whispered Yusuke.

We tracked them as they disappeared.

"Are they dangerous?" I asked.

"A nice breeze can be dangerous."

I contemplated. "If there's a fire you don't want spreading."

Yusuke nodded. I sensed a subtle irritation that he was too wise to let surface.

"If you stay in line, the coyotes—*Canis latrans mearnsi*—they shouldn't be an issue. Our pack is a large one."

"*Canis latrans mearnsi*," I said, repeating the species name. "Where did you learn all of this stuff?"

"A friend of mine gave me a book a while back," said Yusuke, wandering out of line toward a rock formation. He gestured for me to join him, so I did. Behind the rocks was a bush of magnificent white flowers, its petals oscillating in the dry wind. "*Datura wrightii*— they call them the Sacred Datura. Such delicate, graceful little things, aren't they?"

"Very," I said.

"You'd change your mind if you happen to eat one."

"They're poisonous?"

"To the utmost."

I plucked a flower and twirled it in my fingers. "The people who cut. What do you think happens to them?"

He shrugged. "I wouldn't recommend finding out."

As we rejoined the line, Ruth was standing with Li. The two enjoyed a lot of time together, as much as two could enjoy in a line of millions. The four of us watched the sunrise play out in silence. Yusuke and Ruth had always done this—admired the sun—from day one, and Li and I started to participate within a few weeks. For some reason it seemed like the only way to start the day. It was a time when some of the line was still asleep, so you could enjoy standing still, not having to worry about incessantly inching forward. So we would stand there motionless, our hearts fixed to the horizon, and let the light do the talking. I don't know how long these moments lasted. Minutes or years, perhaps, depending on who you asked. As far as I could tell, if you found yourself waiting, a minute became an hour. If you lost yourself waiting, a lifetime became a dream.

"Some say the sun does the same thing every day," said Yusuke.

Only the wind responded. It weaved through the rocks and trees and hills.

I was many years into the line and the sunset was obscured by a cumulus cloud. These were the best sunsets—the imperfect ones. Typically we could see the whole process, the sun descending through the desert's lateral haze and slipping away. But this sunset was different, an anomaly.

"It's been a pleasure getting to know you, Richard," said Ruth.

"Same with you, Ruth."

She turned to Yusuke and said nothing and everything in a caring glance. I realized later that Ruth had coddled me in a way. She would say things that could have been left unsaid, because she was unsure if I'd have *felt* it. Once you grow out of time, the strongest thoughts are ruined by words—you have to *feel* them. She must have known I wasn't there yet.

Ruth and Yusuke stood motionless as the last sliver of light vanished, riding down the backbone of ancient hills. The darkness settled in, and we lay down among the billions.

The next morning Ruth and Li were gone. Vanished. Nowhere to be found in the predawn blue.

"They were too happy to try to cut," I said.

"I agree," said Yusuke.

"Did they say anything to you? Last night."

He shook his head and smiled.

"They kept to themselves a lot recently. It was a little strange," I said. "Maybe they—"

"I don't think it was strange," said Yusuke. "We knew them."

"Yea, and we know they definitely wouldn't cut."

He nodded.

"So what the hell is going on?"

"They mustn't have cut," said Yusuke.

"You think they wandered off?" I scanned the surrounding desert. The air felt less dry. I had been sensing this—the climate was changing very slowly, with each month being a fraction closer to rain. In the distance, miles and miles and years ahead, I could see a large expanse of trees that swallowed the line in its shade.

"Crimson bottlebrushes," said Yusuke.

"What?"

"Those trees, that's what they're called. *Melaleuca citrina*—the crimson bottlebrush. It's—"

"Yusuke, Ruth and Li are gone and you're worried about trees!" I snapped.

"Not worried," he said, his eyes tracking a black-tailed jackrabbit, *Lepus californicus,* through a rock formation. Then, as I panicked, my mind reaching for answers that weren't ready to come, the first morning light materialized. It had Yusuke's full attention.

"I never told you how it happened," he said.

I had asked many times how Yusuke died, but he'd always said the time wasn't right yet. Ruth had explained that she had died of lung cancer, and Li had been killed during an earthquake.

"My wife, Jeanie, she had acute myeloid leukemia for six years," said Yusuke. "To fight, it became her life. Our life. Before she got sick, we had plenty of support. Family, friends, coworkers, the same as most people. But they slowly started to disappear. Some died, but most just stopped coming around. And I don't blame any of them. It's a very hard thing to be around death like that. She wasn't technically dead yet, but it was already there, waiting for us. It's like standing on the train tracks and feeling the rails shake. Right when you feel that first little vibration, it's on its way. But the more you think about it, the more you realize it was always coming. And it's unclear whether you were waiting for it or it was waiting for you."

I felt this so deeply that to agree would have been redundant.

"A few days after she died, I cut my wrists with a steak knife."

A coyote howled, and some others howled back.

"Hopefully Jeanie's not in line anymore," said Yusuke. "But if I had known how this whole thing works—the order of the line—I'd have gotten it over with the moment she stopped breathing so we could have been beside each other out here. That would have changed things."

I stayed silent.

"So you and Li must have died at the same time."

"Right after you," I said.

123

"I came earlier, yes," he said. "Those trees up ahead…"

"*Melaleuca citrina.*"

"The birds love them. We're too far away to see it now, but if I had to guess, they're there, doing what birds do."

Only the stubborn would try to sleep through the morning chorus. Most of us learned to wake up with the birds. Once the chirping started, we would be on our feet, chatting among those beside us in line, our conversations no different from those taking place up in the branches. I wondered if all the birds were dead too: if they were in some kind of avian afterlife. But I realized that nothing about the line was any less alive than the life I'd known before it. For all I knew, this line could very well be the main event—with my time as a steamfitter and a brother and a son being a mere preparatory existence. And there could be another life to come.

Yusuke and I hadn't spoken in quite some time. He'd become the best friend I'd ever had.

Goodnight, my friend, he thought.

Goodnight.

The sunrise was scattered by the crimson bottlebrushes. Rays beamed through the forest's cracks, filling all the spaces that would let daylight in. Mourning doves and loggerhead shrikes and ravens and a thousand other species sang their songs.

The days grew shorter, and I lost track of time.

I had told Yusuke far earlier, when we were still in the desert, that I had no idea how much time was passing, that it didn't really matter to me—but that was a lie. In reality, I was still waiting, tapping a foot in my mind: time still dragged back then, and I often considered eating a Sacred Datura. But I only lied to Yusuke because his stoicism was too pure to ruin. He was so at ease with waiting that to voice my own impatience would have been disrespectful. He had grown out of time. And a small part of me knew that I had to do the same.

Somewhere among the trees, a week or a decade or a lifetime since I first woke up to the chirping birds, as I went to sleep without thinking about any of this, a seagull floated in place, pleasantly motionless against the wind.

I was awakened in the middle of the night for the first time since Mom's fiftieth birthday. There were footsteps. I saw Yusuke calmly walking away from the line, into the darkness of the forest.

I followed him.

Many miles later, we exited the trees into a grassland that slowly turned into towering sand dunes filled with plants and insects neither of us could name. Days became nights became days, but we didn't stop trekking until we heard the waves, just before the sun would be coming up.

This is as far as we can go together.

I'm going back.

It was an assumption. Yusuke smiled.

125

You're a counselor now.

That wasn't your first time in the line…

He shook his head. *My twenty-second. I tried to cut five times, before giving up on finding Jeanie. And I ate a few flowers. So it's more like fourteen. It wasn't until I met Yuri that I had any chance of making it all the way.*

Yuri was your counselor?

He nodded.

So you get sent to the back of the line if you cut. It was a personal thought, so he didn't respond. *Those fourteen times—you were counseling people?*

He nodded. *You were my first to make it. Now I can move on.*

To where?

Yusuke shrugged, then handed me a small leather-bound book.

I read the title: *The Flora and Fauna of the Former.*

The sun popped its head above the sand dunes, so we watched it.

I killed myself too.

Yusuke nodded.

You knew?

He took his eyes off the sunrise and concentrated on me, the center of his universe. *You will learn the life of whomever you end up counseling. It will come to you in your sleep.*

I'll dream about it?

He could sense my confusion. *I wouldn't call it dreaming.*

Some seagulls swooped down overhead, having fun in the wind.

When you get to the back of the line, you are to counsel the person who arrives behind you. You will get to know them in line, but you will be them at night. You will live their first life, their life before the line. You will become more than yourself. And it will feel no different, no less real than any of the lives you'll live.

The seagulls squawked and squealed, then fought the wind toward the coast.

It is futile to try explaining it all. You will only understand when it happens. And just know that they won't all make it, the ones you counsel. It is very rare to make it the first time around like you.

I had a great counselor.

He smiled.

What if I cut now? Or eat a flower? I wanted all the answers.

I'm not sure. I never tried once I became a counselor.

The dune grass moved in unison, like a swaying crowd and the world was a concert.

Yusuke stepped closer to me. *Just know that your life, I know it as well as you. You will be with me always. Since the day I met you in the back of the line, your first life was my life while I was asleep. I was born Richard Michael Tarry. I lived your every moment. And last night, in the forest, that life ended for me the same way it did for you. It was Mom's fiftieth birthday, and the sirens woke us up around three, and we took all those Vicodins, and we thought it was the last thing we'd ever do.*

I began to cry.

He stared me in the eyes and I knew it meant farewell, a parting of ways too deep to have anything to do with what I'd always called *goodbye*. He walked off into the dunes, toward the call of the ocean.

Seagulls beckoned from the coast. I could taste the ocean.

I handed Samara the leather-bound book and walked away across the dunes. It was the hardest thing I ever had to do. Leaving her felt like an impossibility, like separating from my shadow. In the line, she'd been with me for years and years and years. And at night, I was her. I broke her bones. I gasped her lungs. I loved Benjamin. I died in a Rio de Janeiro hospital while a father who never loved me like he loved Martha and Ramon was getting something from the vending machine.

As I climbed dune after dune, I thought of Yusuke. He had walked this very sand. He was me, and I was Samara.

I wouldn't call it dreaming.

The time it took to make it across the sand dunes was between twenty and fifty years. Each day was different though. With every dune I passed, I could feel the sand holding slightly more moisture, the desert fading away. Each day, each dune, each step made me realize the ocean didn't begin or end, not in the way I had once thought.

When I got to the final dune, the beach below was packed with people sitting in neat rows, all dead silent, each of them reading a book. A small jungle separated me from the shore, so I trekked through the vines and the mud, taking a rest on the trunk of a fallen palm tree as I arrived at the beach. I could feel the peoples' thoughts. They were personal thoughts, random and incoherent, the type one has just before falling asleep. Perhaps communication was not allowed here.

Hello, Richard. Yusuke approached from among the silent.

Yusuke!

He held his finger to his lips. I jumped to my feet and hugged him, and he hugged me back. He sat in silence listening to my ramblings and questions and stories about Samara before handing me a blue-covered book. *This is what they're reading.*

I read the title: *The Methods of the Latter.*

He pointed to an empty spot in the rows of people. *That is your spot.*

That's where you were sitting?

He nodded.

Where are you going?

He pointed out across the ocean.

What's out there?

It's where you'll end up, hopefully. If you can be at peace.

A massive wave crashed on the shore, the ocean riding up the beach, kissing peoples' feet.

At peace?

He nodded, gesturing to the book. *When you finish it.*

What does it mean though? At peace.

It cannot be explained. But I agree with it.

So what's out there? In the ocean, where you're going—what is it? Is it another line?

It's most similar to your first life, the one we share. Or Samara's life, the one you lived at night.

So it's like a normal life, but everyone's at peace? I stood up.

He nodded.

Like heaven, essentially?

Not quite.

I paced. *Who set this whole thing up? Who's running it?*

We are.

Who's 'we'?

He gestured for me to stop pacing. *Those of us who are at peace. It's all voted upon. Things change every couple thousand years when someone thinks up an improvement or a tweak to the system. But for the most part, it's been more or less the same for as far back as people can remember. There's our first lives; then there's the line, which we call the Former; then there's this place, the Latter. The Latter used to take place in the mountains. That was the last change to the system, a minor one, about a thousand years ago.*

I sat back down beside him. *So this is all just set up by us? There's no God? Or some kind of higher beings?*

If there was a God, I would hope he'd come up with a better system than this. He chuckled. *We both know*

130

what our first life was like. Nothing to write home about, really. Waiting in line forever? Sitting on a beach for a few thousand years? I hate to be the bearer of bad news, but this system is set up by people just like you and I. And like any other human system, it has its flaws. It's not perfect. But that's why it gets improved every once in a while.

Yusuke felt my devastation. He placed a gentle hand on my back. *It's not as bad as you think.*

I opened the book. Every page was blank. Not a single word anywhere but the cover.

He got to his feet. *It will start to make sense. Not all at once, but eventually. You will see, in your sleep.*

Another life?

Yusuke nodded, his eyes fixed on the ocean. Dolphins patrolled the shallows.

Goodbye, Yusuke.

No need for goodbye, Richard. You will be me tonight.

Which of your lives?

Yusuke walked into the waves, swimming until he was small and blue and ocean himself.

About the Author

Matt Gibson is an independent author from Point Lookout, New York, who would be appalled if this description labeled him as anything grander than a man who sits in chairs and tells stories. He's currently alive, as far as anyone knows, and lives in Long Beach, California.

If you enjoyed this book,
please leave an Amazon review.

Made in the USA
Monee, IL
01 September 2021